MW00612238

Murder Out of Commission

Murder Out of Commission

R. B. DOMINIC

PUBLISHED FOR THE CRIME CLUB BY

DOUBLEDAY & COMPANY, INC.

GARDEN CITY, NEW YORK

1976

All of the characters in this book
are fictitious, and any resemblance
to actual persons, living or dead,
is purely coincidental.

Library of Congress Cataloging in Publication Data

Dominic, R. B.
Murder out of commission.

I. Title.
PZ4.D673Mt3 [PR6054.045] 823'.9'14
ISBN: 0-385-12058-3
Library of Congress Catalog Card Number 76–2768

Copyright © 1976 by Doubleday & Company, Inc.
All Rights Reserved
Printed in the United States of America
First Edition

Murder Out of Commission

CHAPTER 1

The President of the United States lives in Washington, D.C. But so do 746,000 other people, and these days, they have some say about who moves into 1600 Pennsylvania Avenue. The capital of the nation has finally won the right to vote for President. Not that the struggle is over: the District of Columbia still lacks effective representation in Congress.

"And between you and me, Ben, it's a beautiful thought," said the Honorable Anthony Martinelli (D., R.I.), carefully hitching up his flawlessly creased trousers. "Damned near a million people with no poor SOB of a congressman to blame everything on."

Benton Safford (D., Ohio) propped his feet on the desk and locked his hands behind his neck. From his unshined shoes to his rumpled, thinning hair, he was a complete contrast to the bandbox perfection of his colleague.

"Getting a lot of heat from home, Tony?" he asked.

"Every dingbat in town is on my neck!"

"Anything serious?"

"They're cutting back at the Navy Yard."

"I see," said Ben soberly. Ohio may be short on Navy Yards, but from a congressman's perch, one federal installation is like another when closing time comes. Nothing had threatened Ben Safford's long tenure in office more than the shutdown of the Veterans Administration Hospital outside the city of Newburg.

"No, you don't see," Tony corrected him. "I've worked my tail off on this one. I got Defense to phase out instead of chopping. I got the union to play ball. I got the mayor and the papers going along. And what comes out of the woodwork? The

League of Women Voters, for Chrissake! First, they yell at me to cut the defense budget. Then they scream at me to—"

But Safford's voice drowned him out like a foghorn.

"People are yelling and screaming at me, too. Mine are all up in arms about a nuclear power plant." Elaborately casual, he noticed a newcomer. "Oh, hello, Elsie. Come on in and join the party."

Congresswoman Elsie Hollenbach (R., Calif.) was not one of the new breed of women running for office. She had succeeded to her late husband's seat years ago. By now her ramrod back, her unyielding principles and her addiction to worthy causes were part of the Capital Hill landscape. Despite Ben's efforts, she had caught the reference to the League of Women Voters.

"Don't look at me like that, Elsie!" Tony protested. "Just because they're crazy about you doesn't make them perfect."

"The League performs valuable service in informing the electorate." Mrs. Hollenbach spoke with automatic reproach, but her attention was elsewhere. "Did I hear you say something about a nuclear plant, Ben?"

"That's right, Elsie. They're putting one up near Newburg," Ben said over his shoulder. He was already busy with bottles and glasses as his contribution toward soothing friction between colleagues.

Mrs. Hollenbach was famous for her encyclopedic knowledge of the research being conducted by every congressional staff. Accepting her drink, she said thoughtfully, "The Joint Committee on Atomic Energy has issued several reports on private reactor performance. If you're having trouble about a nuclear power plant, Ben, you ought to take a look at them."

"But I'm not having any trouble!"

Martinelli promptly bit the hand that had just given him Bourbon. "You said yourself that you were getting a lot of flack."

"And believe me," said a voice from the doorway, "if you've got anybody thinking about an atom within five hundred miles of your bailiwick, you've got real trouble." Congressman Eugene Valingham Oakes (R., S.D.) lumbered into the room with heavy weariness, heading for the improvised bar. "Make that a double, Ben. I've had a hard, hard day."

Safford and Martinelli were openly skeptical. Val Oakes's ability to sleep through witness after witness was the envy of all. Mrs. Hollenbach's reaction was even more unsympathetic. She was inspired to remember a fact.

"That's right, Val. You're on the Atomic Energy Committee. That means you can bring Ben up to date on safety standards while you're having that drink."

Val Oakes groaned. "Where do you think I've been all this week? Sixty experts, we've listened to," he said bitterly. "Every damn one of them is some kind of scientist. And every damn one of them claims there's about as much chance of getting hurt in a reactor accident as being struck by a meteor. Anybody ever been flattened by a meteor in Newburg, Ben?"

"Not to my knowledge."

"Happens all the time in South Dakota."

There was silence at this ambiguous testimonial to the safety of the nation's nuclear power program. Tony Martinelli was the first to recover.

"There's your line, Ben. Just tell everybody that sixty experts swear your plant is absolutely safe."

"I don't intend to tell anyone anything at all about nuclear power. It's none of my business," Safford said stubbornly. "This outfit, Buckeye Atomic Corporation, has gotten a preliminary okay from the AEC to build a plant in a small town called Murren. The local people are going to have some kind of referendum. It's their decision."

"God help you," said Val devoutly.

Tony was more optimistic. "Oh, look on the bright side. Sure, it's in Ben's district, but it's not downtown Newburg." He paused doubtfully. "That is, if Newburg has a downtown."

Ignoring this slur, Ben continued his explanation. "Murren used to be a railroad stop, but since the freight service was cut, it's been downhill all the way. From what I hear, they're tickled pink to have a nuclear plant. The tax base will be big enough so they can lower their property rate, and they're hoping for some jobs, too. That means a lot, right now."

Elsie demanded clarification. "Yet you said you've been getting protests, Ben."

"Some," he admitted. "From nearby communities."

Tony's dark eyes sparkled with comprehension. "The environmentalists," he said softly. "The save-the-caribou crowd. The League of Women Voters!"

Mrs. Hollenbach rose above this provocation. "The public has good cause to be anxious about the safety of these plants. Naturally, we are all concerned about developing energy alternatives. But that is no excuse to introduce potential hazards throughout the nation."

"I don't know why you aren't argle-bargling with all these eggheads instead of me, Elsie," said Val admiringly.

The explanation was simple. Mrs. Hollenbach was occupied full-time keeping tabs on the Armed Forces, the Attorney General and the Bureau of the Budget. She was also keeping an eye on Ben.

"What," she demanded, "what does Janet say about this?"

Ben shifted. Almost all congressional bachelors have some wifely substitute watching events back home. In Ben's case, his sister, Janet, was his chief political lieutenant and intelligence agent. It was her phone calls, not the letters crossing his desk, that had been causing prickles of unease.

"She says there's a lot of talk in Newburg and Lincolnwood," he evaded.

"Ah ha!"

"But Murren is where Buckeye Atomic has chosen a site, and Murren is happy about it. That lets me off the hook. I don't see any trouble heading my way."

"Then you're looking in the wrong direction," said Elsie tartly. "As I have no doubt Janet has been pointing out to you."

Val Oakes reached into his store of political wisdom for a less personal comment.

"Nothing, Ben, ever lets a congressman off the hook."

*   *

Congressman Safford had long accepted two basic axioms. Val Oakes knew more about politics than anyone else in the world. And Janet knew more about Newburg County, Ohio. He was therefore less surprised than he pretended when, a scant forty-eight hours later, he found himself in the back seat of a car heading for the Murren Grange Hall.

"I still don't see why I'm doing this," he grumbled. "I'm only in town for twenty-four hours, and there are more important things for me to attend to."

"Oh, no, there aren't," his sister retorted. "People are getting pretty excited about this nuclear plant, and it's high time they saw you taking an interest in it, too."

"All they're likely to see is me making a fool of myself. I'm not an atomic scientist. All I can do is parrot what somebody else has said. And if people are all that excited, I'm going to make half of them mad every time I open my mouth."

In the dim light, he could see the back of Janet's head shaking vigorously.

"It's not that kind of issue, Ben," she said. "You'd be surprised at the amount of emotion that's being generated. And when everyone is up in arms about something, the least a congressman can do is show that he notices the problem."

She did not have to labor the point. Watergate was still fresh enough so that every elected official recognized the dangers of ignoring public outrage.

"Go on," said Ben grimly.

"Take Murren, for instance." Here Janet Lundgren was on home ground. Her network of civic committees, women's organizations and charitable activities reached into every nook and cranny of the county. "They were a depressed community even before the economic troubles started. But inflation made it doubly hard for all the old people up there. Then recession came and closed down the soybean press. The offer from Buckeye Atomic seemed like the first light at the end of a long tunnel. But before it got off the ground the environmentalists started up. As far as Murren is concerned, a lot of rich people down in Lincolnwood are ready to kill their only hope, while the politicians stand by and let it happen."

Janet did not provide Ben's only insight into the passions of southern Ohio. Her husband, Fred, was the owner of Lundgren Ford, Newburg's largest automobile dealer. Until now, he had been concentrating on his driving.

"That's fine as far as it goes," he said, making his first contribution, "but you've got to remember that the people in Lincolnwood are scared, too."

"Not about unemployment, they're not," Ben replied with

confidence. The housing developments of Lincolnwood were a product of prosperity. Anyone who lost his job had to leave before the next set of payments came due.

"The young folks are different nowadays. They're all walking medical experts. Honest to God, Ben, they're worried about parts of the human body you and I have never heard of. And it's not a put-on. They're scared stiff about asbestos in the water and the smog content in the air, and the ones around here have added radio-activity to the list. And for all I know, they're right."

Ben was reminded of an earlier conversation. "I wonder if many of them hail from South Dakota," he mused. "Getting pelted with meteors seems to make you skeptical about safety standards."

"Never mind that." As usual Janet was more single-minded than her menfolk. "The point is that as far as Lincolnwood is concerned, twelve hundred people in Murren, simply in order to get a bigger tax base, are willing to risk poisoning half a million people in the county while—"

But Ben could finish the thought himself. "While the politicians stand by and let it happen," he chanted.

"Exactly. So you may make some people mad by what you say, but you'll make them all mad if you stay away. There's a lot of interest being roused."

"There sure is!"

This hearty endorsement came from the driver's seat where Fred was bringing the car to a halt. With an expansive wave, he indicated the long line of red brake lights ahead.

"It must be the first traffic jam in the history of Murren," he said philosophically.

"Do you think it can be?" asked Ben, leaning forward to peer through the twilight.

"Has to be. The turnoff is just past that bend in the road." Fred had swiveled around to fling an arm over the back of the seat with the leisurely air of a man prepared to sit it out.

He was perfectly right. When they finally inched to the head of the line, they found a state trooper funneling cars into the town center with a look of weary resignation.

"You're not going to be able to park near the Grange," he

began before recognition dawned. "Oh, hello, Fred. Isn't this something? They've been piling in for the last hour."

"Who are they all? I thought this was an information night for the voters of Murren."

"Well, the pickets got here first. And then—"

Ben's hackles had already started to rise. "Pickets?"

"Sure thing. Then the reporters came, and a bunch of students from the college. And," concluded the trooper grimly, "every living one of them has come in his own car."

It was clear that to the state police, Murren's big night was simply a traffic obstruction.

"And they're not so far off," grumbled Fred, after it had been necessary to park six blocks away and walk back.

Janet had her own way of looking at things. "The more people here, the sooner everyone will know that Ben turned up," she said sturdily.

They had barely crossed the threshold of the Grange Hall before she began hailing acquaintances. First and foremost was Mrs. Lorraine Westerfeld.

"You remember my brother, Ben Safford, don't you, Lorraine?"

Mrs. Westerfeld beamed. "I ought to. I've filled his tank often enough."

The hearty handshake, even more than the reference, reminded Ben that Murren's only gasoline station was run by the widow of the original owner. It was one of his regular refueling stops during campaign tours.

"Lorraine is a selectman," continued Janet. "She's the one behind this information night."

"George Barry and I did it together, so everyone could get the facts. God knows we've had plenty of opinions! But it will make all the difference, having you here, Mr. Congressman. People in Murren were beginning to think it was them against the world."

Within minutes this view was being repeated by George Barry. Short, round, and pugnacious, he was less polite than Mrs. Westerfeld.

"Wondered if we were ever going to see one of our elected reps," he began. "Congratulations! The boys in the state legislature are all hiding out in Columbus. Just because that bunch out there can swing a lot of votes."

He stabbed his cigar at the front doors, through which the pickets could be seen, circling the town green slowly and steadily.

Ben said that he figured he could use information on Murren's reactor program just as much as anyone else.

"Not everybody wants information," snorted Barry as he turned to go. "Those people out there, they act like they've got a pipeline direct to God."

Janet was already preening herself on the basis of these two encounters, but the third was her real triumph. A slim girl crossing the lobby brushed against them, started to apologize, then did a double take. Her face lit up.

"You're Congressman Safford, aren't you?" she said eagerly. "I'm Abby Carr, and it's simply wonderful to find you here. Only this morning Paul was saying that it's criminal the way the politicians are trying to side-step this issue."

"Paul?" asked Safford, totally at sea.

"My husband. He's chairman of PEP," she explained in a rush. "Could you possibly wait a minute while I get him? He'll be thrilled to see our protests are finally getting some official response."

Without waiting for a reply she darted through the doors and down into the street.

"I suppose that's the opposition," Ben murmured in a careful undertone.

"PEP is short for a Pure Environment for Posterity," said Janet who always seemed to know these things. "They organized the pickets outside. And I was right about everybody being pleased by your coming."

Ben shook his head gloomily. "They're pleased so far. But sooner or later, someone's going to want more than my body. They're going to want me to take a position."

The moment seemed at hand. Abby Carr reappeared, pulling forward a tall, intense-looking young man. He was much less enthusiastic than his wife.

"Of course we're glad our congressman showed up," he said

grudgingly. "But I hope you haven't come to give us more of that Washington pap about how safe these reactors are."

Choosing his words with care, Safford replied, "I'm not here to tell anyone anything. I'm no scientist. You have to be qualified to understand the technical data—"

"Technical data!" Paul Carr said scornfully. "That's the shield they keep trying to hide behind. You don't have to be an expert to understand right from wrong. Everybody knows they keep having accidents with these nuclear piles. That's a fact you can't get away from, no matter how hard they try to distort the truth with statistics and tables. The membership of PEP has turned out tonight to demonstrate that we're not sitting still for another Washington snow job. We intend . . ."

As he continued, Ben Safford breathed a sigh of relief. It was a piece of luck that this young man was a born lecturer. Paul Carr was far too busy sounding off himself to care what his congressman thought. But there was curiosity mingled with gratitude. Someone in Washington was regarded by PEP as the enemy. Ben wondered if he would ever be told who that was.

CHAPTER 2

It took almost two hours to find out. In the interval, the audience heard a number of speakers fill their allotted time. Lorraine Westerfeld led the way with a survey of Buckeye Atomic's impact on town financing. Nobody listening to her painstaking recital would have called her an inspired speaker. She didn't have to be.

". . . will result in lowering the tax rate by fifteen dollars the thousand," she read slowly.

When property owners get that kind of news, they are not fussy about oratorical style.

George Barry, who came next, also discussed economics. But he had not done his homework. He was short on facts and figures and long on generalities. He applauded the construction jobs to come, and he liked even better the employment picture in an operating facility. Buckeye Atomic would create over a hundred clerical and maintenance positions.

"Of course," he conceded, "the bulk of the technical spots will go to physicists and engineers who are out-of-towners. But they won't be out-of-towners for long. And they'll bring Murren just the kind of people we want."

With that, the local concerns of Murren were left behind. Sheridan Ireland, introduced as the president of Buckeye Atomic, dealt with the energy needs of southern Ohio. The utility companies would not be able to meet the demand with existing installations.

"And if new generators are necessary," he growled somberly,

"it doesn't make sense to have them dependent on foreign oil. You all know what that can mean to your electricity bills."

The trouble came with the fourth speaker. He was a safety inspector working for the Atomic Energy Commission, but he sounded more like a bookkeeper than an engineer. Settling his gold-rimmed glasses firmly on his nose, he began to tick his points off, one by one. First, there was no appreciable radiation hazard from a nuclear power plant operating normally.

"Less than from having your dentist take an X ray," he reassured them.

But what about an accident, what about a uranium pile running out of control? Well, that was where the AEC came in. Not only did the Commission oversee the original design of each reactor, it insisted on a safety system, a backup system, and then a backup for the backup. Constant tests were a feature of the AEC's vigilance.

Paul Carr was on his feet before Inspector Davis Quentin finished inviting questions from the floor.

"You propose putting a nuclear threat in our back yard, and that's all the information you're going to give us?" he asked. "When we hear about breakdowns and radioactive leakage every day?"

Unflustered, Inspector Quentin said he would be happy to provide figures. The AEC was justifiably proud of its safety record. That indeed was the heart of his argument. There might be breakdowns, but there had never been any danger. The primary systems worked and the backup systems had never been called upon.

"My God, what good are a bunch of AEC statistics?" Carr said sarcastically. "Everybody knows you've sold out to the power companies, and they're not going to let us have the truth. They lied about the fuel-price adjustment, and they'll lie about nuclear perils as long as it's worth their while."

"Mr. Carr, I assure you—"

"Look at Mr. Ireland!" Carr pointed an accusing finger at the platform. "He's hiding behind the title of president of Buckeye. But how many of you know that he's really chairman of the board at Tristate Consolidated Electric? And that they own over half of Buckeye Atomic?"

Davis Quentin refused to be drawn into side issues. He droned away at his target. "The Commission compiles its data on a nationwide basis and has been doing so for over fifteen years. Its figures are regularly reviewed by the Joint Committee in Congress and also by the press."

His coolness goaded Paul Carr into a frenzy. "For all practical purposes, you've been hired by Sheridan Ireland to give us a whitewash job," he raged.

Gobbling like a turkey cock, Ireland hurled himself into the fray. "Look here, I don't know who you are but you can't say things like that. You don't know what you're talking about."

"You just try and stop me saying what I want!"

"Since when do you know more than the—"

"Mr. Carr, the records of the AEC—"

BANG! BANG! BANG! Lorraine Westerfeld was wielding her gavel like a blacksmith. She did not stop until the disputants were silenced. When she spoke she was ominously calm. "Mr. Carr, we haven't invited speakers here for them to stand up and be insulted."

"If my questions are offensive to the inspector, it's because of his situation," the young man retorted hotly.

Lorraine swept on as if he had not spoken. "Particularly by people who have no right to be here."

"What do you mean?" Carr was taken aback. "This meeting is open to the public."

"Oh, no it isn't. The notice says plainly that it's open to all residents of Murren. You don't qualify, so I'm asking you to leave."

"I don't remember anything about being a Murren resident."

"It's the line at the bottom. There's a copy of the notice on the front door. You can read it," Lorraine smiled grimly, "on your way out."

For a moment it looked as if Paul Carr would argue the point. Then he jerked his chin angrily at his wife and muttered, "Come on, honey. We're getting out of this rigged showpiece."

Abby, who must have weighed ninety pounds dripping wet, stalked martially down the center aisle—shoulders back, eyes straight ahead and two angry red spots on her cheeks. Her husband shrugged with assumed nonchalance and brought up the rear.

As Lorraine Westerfeld placidly watched the departure of the Carrs, Ben Safford realized that she had all the politician's instinct to see only what she wanted to see. Over half the seats in the Grange Hall were occupied by non-residents, and they were all receiving Mrs. Westerfeld's message loud and clear. If outsiders wanted to sit and listen, fine! If they tried to derail the proceedings, it was the old heave-ho.

From the sounds that soon came filtering through the windows, it seemed that Paul Carr was relaying this message to his supporters. There were shouts and jeers followed by the methodical rhythm of a steady chant. As it swelled in volume, Mrs. Westerfeld continued her show of force.

"We'll have those windows closed and I'd like to welcome our next speaker," she said in one breath. "He is Roger Gladstone from Lomax Tool and he designed the reactor that Buckeye Atomic will use. Four Lomax reactors are already generating electricity at other sites throughout the Midwest."

For the first time that evening, Murren got a dose of genuine, passionate enthusiasm. Soaring far above the immediate requirements of Newburg County, Gladstone predicted a future in which all power needs, from transportation to heavy manufacturing, would be met by atomic energy.

"Not since the water wheel has mankind been offered such a clean, non-contaminating fuel," he said, impatiently brushing aside a lock of dark hair that kept falling over his brow.

According to Roger Gladstone, the smokestacks of industry would soon be a thing of the past.

"Dollar for dollar, radioactive ores are more than competitive with oil, coal and gas."

According to Roger Gladstone, you could stick a spade in anywhere and shovel the stuff up.

Ben had met this kind of dedication before. As a result, he no longer believed in that brave new world where everything is clean and beautiful and cheap. But Roger Gladstone was obviously a font of information and more than willing to share his knowledge. Accordingly, when the speeches were over and refreshments served, Ben zeroed in on Gladstone.

He did not have much competition. Quite a lot of people wanted to talk to Mrs. Westerfeld about the tax rate, and plenty were tackling Sheridan Ireland about last summer's brownout. Only one scatterbrained lady challenged him for Gladstone's attention.

"Oh, I was so glad to hear what you said about cars," she dithered. "The present system simply has to go."

As if a button had been pushed, Gladstone began to recite statistics about smog concentration in urban areas.

". . . in the last ten years, respiratory diseases have increased by more than seventy per cent, Mrs. Tibbs," he was saying earnestly when she interrupted.

"We don't have any smog in Murren," she said. "I was talking about how I'm always running out of gas on Route 118. Now, would I have to keep filling the tank on one of your nuclear cars?"

Ben admired the way Gladstone shifted gears without blinking an eye. By the time Mrs. Tibbs had been sped on her way, Gladstone had gained one more adherent to his cause.

"Would you believe it?" he asked with a grin that took years off his age. "I'm asked that question every time I speak. It makes you wonder how the country can have so many cars on the road if nobody ever remembers to buy gas."

"You probably get asked my questions, too," said Safford ruefully. "But with everyone in Newburg County raising a storm about this reactor, I'd better know something about it."

The next ten minutes were profitable for Ben. He found out about past experience with commercial generating plants, the initial capacity of Buckeye, the area it would service, the kilowatt-hour cost and plans for future expansion. Gladstone was promising to send him copies of various reports when their tête-à-tête was interrupted.

Sheridan Ireland had not enjoyed meeting his customers and was ready to do some criticizing of his own. A choleric flush had spread over his bald pate.

"For God's sake, Roger," he growled. "I thought we agreed you were going to talk about generating electricity. What made you go haring off onto all that other stuff? Think of the harm you may be doing."

Gladstone frowned. "What harm? I was talking about the future of nuclear energy."

"Use your head!" Ireland lowered his voice. "You start blabbing about nuclear cars and Mrs. Westerfeld runs a gas station!"

The trouble with Ireland, Ben decided, was that he was used to dealing with employees who had to take him seriously. Roger Gladstone simply laughed. Then, at exactly the right moment, someone left the building and through the open door came the sounds of a milling crowd with shouts and jeers and orders to get back.

"I don't think Mrs. Westerfeld is your main problem," said Gladstone dryly.

It was a timely reminder to Ben that he should placate a few constituents himself. With a wave to Gladstone he headed across the floor to the refreshment table where his sister was sending up signals.

"You've met Inspector Quentin, haven't you, Ben? Emily Coughlin and I were just thanking him for his talk," Janet said brightly.

Ben looked at her reproachfully. Why did Janet always assume that he had to be nudged about names in his district? He decided to teach her a lesson.

"I'll thank him myself as soon as I've loaded a plate. I haven't forgotten the lemon cake that the Baptist ladies in Murren make."

Emily Coughlin bridled happily and insisted on personally serving him with some of the yellow concoction she was so proud of.

"And you, Mr. Quentin? Just a little more?"

"I wish I could," said Quentin with a show of regret. "But I'm afraid I have to leave now. I have to catch the plane back to Washington."

"What a nice man," said Mrs. Coughlin as he departed. "I hope he doesn't have any trouble outside. You know the state police are here?"

Janet pointed out that the patrol car had been directing traffic since before the meeting started.

Mrs. Coughlin's lips folded firmly. "I still think it's terrible. What right do they have to try and burst in on our meeting? We don't need outsiders telling us what to do."

Ben knew he was going to hear this sentiment repeated in

many forms. As far as Murren was concerned, its zoning problems were its own. Unfortunately, quite a lot of people in greater Newburg could already see disaster. He decided to practice walking the fine line.

"Of course they have no right to take part in your referendum or to disrupt your meeting," he said, on the principle of always beginning with agreement. "What they should have done was hold their own meeting."

Mrs. Coughlin sniffed. "Catch those hooligans doing anything as tame as that!"

Janet had her own strategy for this kind of situation. Whenever the threat of disagreement between Ben and one of his constituents loomed, she enlarged the group. Nine times out of ten someone else would do Ben's dirty work for him.

"Reverend Baines!" she cried across the coffee urn. "Do you know what's going on outside? Emily thinks those protesters may be getting out of hand."

She could not have chosen better, Ben thought appreciatively. Reverend Baines was a veteran of many protests himself.

"Nonsense!" he said heartily. "A very well-conducted group. I've just been out there speaking with them. No one can deny that they have a very legitimate interest in the outcome of our debates. And I for one think . . ."

He stopped at the sound of breaking glass. Instinctively everyone turned to the kitchen door, but there white-aproned helpers were curiously looking out. Before the confusion could be expressed in words, the next crash came, followed by a fusillade. Glass was being shattered all over Murren.

George Barry scrambled up to the podium to tell them why.

"Those PEP troublemakers are going on the rampage," he announced. "They started out by smashing the drugstore window. Now they're doing the rounds of the whole town. I say, let's give the troopers a hand!"

By now the whole room was in movement. Half of those present were backing away from the windows. The other half followed Barry to the door. A speaking look from Janet told Safford his duty.

"JUST A MOMENT!" he bellowed. "This is just a temporary

disruption. The police can handle it, but the fewer people they have to deal with, the better."

He was only partially successful in stemming the tide, but he had given the police the time they needed. Before he finished, a state trooper was in the doorway, propelling a few men from the porch back into the room.

"There's nothing to worry about, folks. It's already over and the people outside have agreed to go home. Let's give them a chance to clear out." He was blocking the exit bodily but the sound of revving motors told its own story. "Things just got out of hand for a couple of minutes. Now you move on back there. You're not going to be able to get your cars out of the lot for a while anyway . . ."

Among those swept back inside was Roger Gladstone, who strolled over to the table, saying, "Well, I might as well have a cup of coffee while I wait."

It was the right note to strike. The melodrama dissolved and everybody began talking to everybody else.

"This is some district you've got, Congressman," said Gladstone, stirring sugar calmly. "Lomax has put in four other reactors and we never had people starting a riot."

"Oh, come on," said Ben. "How much of a riot is it? Did you get far enough to see?"

Gladstone raised a hand in surrender. "I didn't get further than the porch, but all I saw was some people getting into cars. They looked pretty sheepish to me."

"I should think so," said Janet crisply. "The Carrs aren't going to gain much support by smashing windows."

"It probably wasn't them." Ben shrugged. "You know how these things go, Janet. The shindig was enough to attract every teen-ager for miles."

Mrs. Coughlin took a down-to-earth approach. "And who's going to pay for the broken windows? If my car has been damaged, I'll send the bill to those Carrs. And I'll advise everybody else to do the same."

This proposal was an immediate hit with George Barry, still spoiling for action. "You don't have to bother, Emily. The minute they let us out of here, I'll make a survey of the damage," he said fussily. "The selectmen will send the bill, and I hope it's a whopper."

"Do that!" Ben was in favor of any non-violent program. "It may make them think twice about a second demonstration."

"Oh, I think they've had their lesson," Roger Gladstone reasoned. "For a minute there, I thought maybe we were in for real trouble. But, thank God, it's over and no harm done."

Ben remembered those words half an hour later when he and his family were released from Grange Hall to tramp back to the car. As they were passing the darkened Westerfeld Texaco Station, they heard a stifled groan and saw with surprise a dim figure clutching one of the pumps.

"Why, it's George Barry!" exclaimed Fred.

"Are you all right? Do you need—" began Janet, when the figure straightened and flapped a hand to keep her back.

"It's not me, it's that inspector," Barry gasped. "The poor guy got in the way of one of those rocks. God, I'm going to be sick again."

He clutched blindly for support as another spasm gripped him. Then his voice, weak but furious, sounded clearly. "Those damn fools have killed him."

It was almost one o'clock in the morning before the Lund-grens and Ben finally made it back to their living room. Fred took three steps to an easy chair, dragged a hassock forward with the heel of his shoe, hoisted both legs and let them collapse with a thump.

"Oof! What a night!" he grunted. "All things considered, Ben, it's a shame Janet talked you into going out to Murren."

"Uh-huh," said Ben, mindful of the fact that Fred, too, had been dragged out in the best interests of Congressman Safford. "But I don't know. There's bound to be a lot of publicity. And everybody is sure going to know I was there."

Janet did not bother defending herself. Instead she examined her menfolk. Fred's eyes were closed. Ben had reversed a wooden chair, straddled it, and was staring sightlessly into the empty fire-place. Neither of them showed the slighest inclination to head to-ward bed. She sighed.

"Do you want anything to eat? I could fix something."

Any suggestion of food or drink received careful consideration from Fred, who waged an unending battle with his waistline.

"I'm not hungry," he decided, faintly surprised. "But I sure am thirsty. Do we have any beer in the house?"

Within five minutes, Janet had effected some improvement. Fred had revived sufficiently to cradle the frosted can in his hands. Ben's eyes were focusing.

"Did you get anything out of the cops, Fred?" he asked.

From a politician's point of view, Fred's Ford agency was a fair substitute for the general store of yesteryear. Anybody in the county who missed Janet at her clubs, guilds and benefits was bound to turn up at Fred's, looking for a lube job.

"Tommy Youngman's in charge," he began.

"Carolyn's brother?" Janet checked automatically. "I thought he was in the service."

"He got out three years ago, and joined the State Police. Doing real well, his father says. He's had a couple of promotions."

"I didn't know that," said Janet. "Carolyn's back from the Coast, you know. Her husband got transferred."

Ben waited patiently. When you run for office every two years, these things are important.

"Anyway," Fred went on, "Tommy says it looks pretty much the way you'd expect. Lorraine Westerfeld's house is in back of her service station. Inspector Quentin drove directly there about an hour before the meeting. He had a drink with some of the selectmen and they all walked over to the Grange together. When he left to catch his plane, he was cutting around the station to get back to his car. That must have been when things got out of hand. Because there was a big rock, covered with blood, next to his smashed head."

"But surely those PEP people weren't trying to hit anybody," Janet objected. "They were breaking windows, that's all. A lot of people were leaving the Grange and nobody else was hurt."

"Wilma Kirby says she was just missed on her way to her car," Fred reported.

"Wilma Kirby would say anything to get attention!"

Her husband and brother knew better than to attack this feminine appraisal.

"Do they know what set off the rock throwing?" Ben asked, prudently changing the subject.

"Oh, yes. Carr made quite a speech after he was thrown out—about how the reactor was being railroaded through by a lot of people in Ireland's pay. That got everybody going. For a while they just marched around, yelling. Then somebody got the bright idea of making a mock mushroom cloud. When they were done with it, they wanted to hoist it up the flagpole on the Common. But a bunch of Murren teen-agers had seen what was going on and they surrounded the pole. The two groups were shouting a lot of names at each other, the cops were keeping them apart, and out of nowhere, the first rock came flying. As a matter of fact, it broke the window of the pizza parlor. Well, you know the sound of shattering glass acts on some people like a fire siren. Before the cops could do anything, there was a whole barrage."

"But if the police were right there, they must have seen what happened to Inspector Quentin," said Janet.

"That's just the problem. There were lights in front of the Grange and the troopers were concentrating on stopping the trouble. They couldn't see what was going on in the dark a couple of blocks away. They figure someone on the fringe of the crowd let loose with a couple of rocks at the service station just because he couldn't be seen."

Ben grounded his can discontentedly. "Well, it's a mess, no matter how you look at it. I suppose Barry was checking the amount of damage when he stumbled on the body."

"He thought he'd finished. He'd left his car at Lorraine's, too. That's why he started at the other end of town and circled around to the gas station."

George Barry was no favorite with Janet. "He's always talking about making Murren a bigger, livelier place," she commented. "I hope this satisfies him."

"I heard that crack of his about bringing in a better class of people," Ben recalled. "Who is he, anyway?"

Fred chuckled indulgently. "Just another one of those real estate agents. He's got an office in Newburg over on Chapel Street, but he lives in Murren."

"And he's always complaining the town has too many people living on Social Security. He'd like to see a country club there," Janet amplified. "And I suppose if they get enough physicists and engineers, he will."

Ben had no difficulty following Barry's reasoning. "And if there's any kind of housing development up there, he'll be in on the ground floor."

"Sure thing," said Fred cheerfully. "He's the only real estate agent with connections in Murren."

"He's the only one so far." Janet was always realistic. "Oh, dear, it would be nice to think that this accident would make the Carrs quiet down, but it won't. They'll probably try to capitalize on it."

Ben cocked an eyebrow. "Do you know something about the Carrs that I don't?" he asked.

The question was a formality. Of course Janet did.

"They bought a house in Lincolnwood about two years ago. Abby is a nice enough girl. She's a social worker at the hospital and I've run into her on cases several times."

There was a long silence.

"And Paul?" Ben finally prodded.

"Paul is a lawyer," Janet said forebodingly. She could have been reporting a record of armed robberies.

Ben grinned at his sister affectionately. So that was the worm in the apple. Janet regarded any young lawyer in the public eye as simply limbering up to run against her brother in the next election. By now quite a lot of them had.

"Why not give young Carr the benefit of the doubt?" he suggested. "Maybe he's genuinely worried about the environment. After all, it is a mess."

But this was one subject on which Janet was never playful. "Six months ago nobody had heard of him. Now he's building a real following in Lincolnwood and Curryville."

"Then he'd better watch his step. From what I've seen of the people in Lincolnwood and Curryville, they don't like their protests to end up with a corpse."

Janet wrinkled her brow. "Of course, that's true enough. But he'll try to turn things around. You know, a lot of his people were genuinely shocked to find they wouldn't have any say about Buckeye's reactor—that it was all up to the town of Murren. And Lorraine didn't help things any by throwing the Carrs out tonight. She just underlined the fact that in Murren other people don't even have the right to ask questions."

"Carr was a pain in the ass," Fred objected.

Janet waved this aside. "I know he was. But nobody's going to care what he was saying, or how he was saying it. All they'll remember is that he was thrown out—just because he lives in Lincolnwood. That's strike one for Murren. Down in Lincolnwood they think they have just as much right to stand and be counted as Lorraine Westerfeld or George Barry. Now, if Paul Carr plays his cards right, he can come up with strike two. It won't be PEP's protest that ended up with a corpse, not the way he'll tell it. He can make it look as if Murren is some sort of Harlan, Kentucky—a place where the locals settle things with blood and rocks and killing people."

Ben was always willing to listen to Janet on public opinion in Newburg. But this time she was overlooking something.

"That's okay except for one thing. Paul Carr was starting a shouting match with Davis Quentin when he was bounced from the Grange. It doesn't matter if that didn't have anything to do with the accident. There's going to be a lot of sympathy for Quentin as the innocent bystander who got killed when a lot of rowdies let loose—whether they came from Murren or Lincolnwood. If Carr has got any sense, he's going to go very slow on his last exchange with Quentin."

"I only hope you're right," said Janet, making it clear that she did not think so. She started to roam the room shaking pillows and emptying ash trays. "And if you still mean to catch the morning plane, I think it's time we all got some sleep."

Fred was on his feet, but lingering.

"On the whole," he said, "it's a damn good thing you're heading back to Washington tomorrow morning. There's bound to be a lot of feeling about what happened to Quentin. But it'll die down pretty soon. The poor guy wasn't from around here, and that'll make a difference."

It was true. A widow and orphans in Bethesda, Maryland, made things easier for everybody.

"Then we'll be back where we started," said Ben grumpily. "With the Carrs and half of Newburg raising hell out in Murren."

"They can't raise hell for long," Fred told him. "The Murren referendum comes up next week, and after that—well, what can anybody do? Ireland told me that once they get the go-ahead, they're starting construction on Buckeye pronto. Just lie low until then and you shouldn't have too much trouble. God knows you've had to do it before."

Ben could not share Fred's guarded optimism.

"I wouldn't put it past the Carrs and their pals to blockade the building site and expect me to protect their constitutional right to riot in public!"

Fred yawned hugely. "You may be right. But that's down the road. In the short haul, it looks to me as if you're home free. Just keep a low profile until after the referendum, and Buckeye shouldn't cause you any worry at all."

It looked that way to Ben, too. But not for long.

CHAPTER 4

The blow fell two days later. First to feel it was the Atomic Energy Commission.

"Would you mind repeating that?" The big smile that was Andrew Heisse's hallmark faded abruptly.

Stolidly the FBI agent obeyed. "The autopsy report doesn't leave any room for doubt. Davis Quentin's death was no accident. Somebody picked up a rock and smashed it into Quentin's skull—twice. He was murdered!"

Professional training kept Agent Unsell's true feelings masked. Andy Heisse's subordinates were not so well-schooled. Jim Vorhees and Nina Yeager exchanged a quick look. Then Nina tried to keep the proceedings from bogging down.

"That's why the FBI has requested permission to examine Quentin's office and files. We"—Miss Yeager was an AEC attorney—"we don't have any objection. We do want to be present, to be sure classified material is properly handled."

Since Nina Yeager was a long-legged, tawny blonde, Agent Unsell looked gratified and kept his comments about top secret material and leaks to himself.

But she had gone too fast for her boss.

"Quentin wasn't murdered here in Washington," Heisse said stubbornly. "He got himself killed down in . . . in . . ."

"Murren, Ohio," Jim Vorhees supplied.

"Murren, Ohio," Heisse said with a snap. "That's where the FBI should be looking. What do they expect to find here? While I'm a commissioner, I'm not inviting the FBI to nose through the AEC files on fishing expeditions!"

"Mr. Commissioner—"

"Mr. Heisse . . ." Unsell began.

"Now, Andy," said Vorhees in a slow, Georgia drawl. "The FBI understands our special situation—"

"I doubt it!"

Andy Heisse was probably right. The Atomic Energy Commission, which has grown to include the Nuclear Regulatory Commission and the Energy Research and Development Administration, is responsible for everything from uranium mines to nuclear submarines. Most people understand only a fraction of its problems. Congress, for interest, concentrates on the billions of taxpayer dollars the agency handles. Gamblers in Nevada worry about tremors from underground test sites. The Pentagon wants bigger and better warheads.

But there are other headaches, including Roger Gladstone's peacetime uses of atomic energy. Every Buckeye Atomic represents a delicate balance between public and private interests, between safety and progress. And the AEC is always caught in the middle.

That was why Commissioner Heisse was balking. The technical staff claimed that he had no qualifications for his job. But, when it came to defending the AEC against all comers—including the FBI—an ex-lieutenant-governor of California could beat a Nobel-prize winner any day.

"Sure, Dave Quentin was killed down in Ohio," Vorhees continued persuasively. "But he was one of our safety inspectors, Andy. The sooner this murder is cleared up, the better for us. There's probably nothing here at headquarters that will help much. But it's the least we can do."

For all his faults, Heisse was a good listener, especially when a Deputy Commissioner spoke. "Sons-of-bitches," he growled. "Okay, Jim. But I want you sitting in, too, as well as Nina here. And I want you to report back to me. And"—he shot an icy look at Unsell—"I'll be talking to your director. I don't want to read about any sensational discoveries in the newspapers. Understand?"

Unsell and Vorhees took this in stride, Unsell because he had the full measure of FBI self-possession, Vorhees because understanding commissioners was part of his job. Not so Nina Yeager.

"You can see we're all heart here at the AEC, Mr. Unsell," she said mockingly once they had cleared Heisse's office.

Jim Vorhees was almost old enough to be her father. "Don't talk like that, Nina," he chided. "Andy himself went out to Bethesda to break the news to Mrs. Quentin. And he's pushing the pension right through . . . here we are, Mr. Unsell."

Agent Unsell had not traveled all the way to the suburbs to discover that the AEC, like every other government organization, was not always one big happy family. Looking around Davis Quentin's spare cubicle, he said, "Before I get started in here, I've got a few questions."

He had to speak quickly to catch Jim Vorhees.

"Oh, sure," said Vorhees, turning from the door. "I just thought Miss Yeager here could . . . well, anything you want."

Agent Unsell wanted it all. He started with Davis Quentin's job description.

"He was one of our safety inspectors," Vorhees responded. He spent about half his time touring the country, inspecting all existing nuclear power installations, to be sure they meet safety standards—"

"He was a GS-15," Miss Yeager broke in. This meant that Quentin was a highly qualified, highly paid specialist.

Vorhees confirmed this. "He had degrees in physics and architectural engineering."

Unsell nodded. "Then what was he doing in Murren? That sounds more like a public relations job to me."

"It was," said Nina Yeager who had perched on a corner of the desk. "But the AEC tries to be responsive whenever there is legitimate public concern about proposed power plants."

This time it was Vorhees who went beyond the official line. "The real reason Quentin went there was penny pinching," he said, shaking his head sadly. "I checked with Special Services as soon as you called. Quentin was supposed to be on a field trip through Indiana and Kentucky and downstate Illinois. When Buckeye asked for a speaker, Special Services told Quentin to make a detour and squeeze it in. It wasn't far off his route—and it saved sending someone out from headquarters."

"Besides," said Nina Yeager with an enigmatic smile, "Dave loved spreading the gospel. He was a true believer."

"Cut it out!" Vorhees said shortly. "The man's dead. You can stop riding him now."

"I'm not riding him. Dave and I agreed to disagree a long, long time ago," she answered smoothly.

Agent Unsell saw no more was coming. "So, it was just a coincidence that Davis Quentin was in Murren that night? If he hadn't been in the area, you would have sent a speaker from Washington, right?"

"We've got a whole section called Community Relations," Miss Yeager said. "They're always giving speeches."

"And if he hadn't been killed in Murren, Quentin would have proceeded back here to headquarters. And then—"

"No," Vorhees interrupted to contradict. "Dave was in the middle of his tour. He wasn't due back here for another week."

Unsell tapped his pencil on the desk top. Then: "Who did Quentin report to?"

"Why, me," said Vorhees, surprised. "That is, Don Barnes is chief of the Standards Division. But Don reports to me—and I report to the commissioners."

"Get Don Barnes in here," said Agent Unsell, shedding his politeness.

But Don Barnes could not help him any more than Jim Vorhees, Nina Yeager or the department secretaries. The net result was to add one more question to the long list of questions already surrounding the murder.

Why had Inspector Davis Quentin gone to a pay phone in the basement of the Murren Grange to call the Newburg Airport and make a reservation?

Not to Chicago, St. Louis or any other point connecting with southern Illinois where he was supposed to go—but to Washington, D.C.?

*   *

News that Davis Quentin had been murdered got to Murren a step ahead of the FBI.

"Nobody here even knew him," said Lorraine Westerfeld incredulously. Automatically she wiped the dip stick. "He told me himself this was his first trip to Newburg County. Somebody just upped and killed a total stranger."

"It doesn't make sense." George Barry circled the hood and watched Lorraine unscrew the battery caps. "But he wasn't robbed or anything like that."

Crime was not unknown in Murren, but muggers were. Still, both Lorraine and George read the papers and watched TV.

"Why hit him twice? Why not grab his wallet and run?" she asked reasonably. "You're a little low, George. Pass me the water can, will you?"

George had already reached the conclusion that the FBI was working on. "He was killed because of Buckeye."

"People don't turn into murderers over something like that!" she snapped.

"They didn't steal his money," Barry shot back. "Hell, they didn't even steal his briefcase. Tommy says they just riffled through it—then threw it away. What else can it be but Buckeye?"

Lorraine still did not like it. "Sure, those Newburg and Lincolnwood people are against the reactor," she argued. "But what good would killing Inspector Quentin do them? The AEC will just send out another man."

"That's what I'm saying," Barry said, taking the water can that dangled from Lorraine's hand and putting it back next to the pump. "They're crazy—but they're not crazy enough to try scaring off the U. S. Government. The way I see it, they're trying to scare us."

"Us?" Lorraine echoed blankly. "You mean Murren? Oh, come on, George. All this will do is set people's backs up."

"You know that," Barry said flatly, "and I know it. But do you think Paul Carr does? Hell, he brings a bunch of longhairs up here, starts a riot, tries to break up our meeting—"

"They didn't try to break up our meeting," Lorraine interrupted firmly. "They tried to take part. We threw them out."

Barry was not stopping for non-essentials. "Then they started heaving rocks, and when that wasn't exciting enough, they beat the brains out of one of the speakers." He pointed at the ground beneath their feet. "Jesus Christ, Lorraine, the body was lying right there."

Appalled, Lorraine stared at him. Talk like this could make a lot of trouble in a small town.

"We've got to keep everybody calmed down," she began.

"And we're not even sure they knew it was Quentin," Barry continued implacably. "The meeting was breaking up. Maybe they thought he was one of us!"

"Oh, God," Lorraine prayed fervently. "Please keep Carr and all the rest out of Murren—just for a while!"

Her prayer was at least partly answered. The neat dark sedan that pulled up behind George's Oldsmobile had U. S. Government plates. And the two young men who emerged, credentials in hand, did not resemble protesters.

They listened to George Barry's theory with more patience than Lorraine had shown. Then: "That's very interesting, sir. But for the present we have orders to proceed on the assumption that somebody wanted to murder Inspector Quentin."

George Barry simply repeated himself. "That," he said with no hesitation, "doesn't make any sense!"

CHAPTER 5

The FBI descended on Tristate Electric, in Cincinnati, too. After their departure, Sheridan Ireland reacted predictably. He called a meeting of the company executives.

"Well, now we know we're dealing with a murderer," he said, looking around the table imperiously. "All right, what's our tactical response?"

There was a dead silence that would have lasted longer if the conference had been composed entirely of Tristate employees. But the company lawyer had other clients and other claims on his time.

"We're going to have to play it by ear, Sherry."

Ireland swiveled toward him. "If you mean back off—that's out! We're not the first atomic power plant in—"

"There are nuclear power stations all over the country," the lawyer agreed. "There have been for years. But until this week, not a single AEC man has been murdered!"

This was no comfort to Ireland. "Why us! Why us!"

"The environmental movement has boomed," said the lawyer reflectively. "And protesters picked up some pretty strange habits during the Vietnam War. You could say that we're inheriting all that."

"Fine!" said Ireland with sarcasm. "So, we're inheriting the Vietnamese mess. That doesn't help me decide what to do!"

"I doubt if you should do anything."

Ireland's savagery made the whole table stir. "Listen, Tristate's whole expansion program is geared to Buckeye. We need more capacity—and where the hell are we going to get it? A bunch of

nuts decide to run wild, they murder a government man—and
you tell me to do nothing!"

He was almost spitting when he came to a halt, more because
he had run out of steam than because of the lawyer's raised hand.

"Sherry, you're looking at this the wrong way." He ignored
the deep-throated growl. "Forget the murder for a minute." He
looked around for support. "You boys did a pretty good job
selling Buckeye, didn't you?"

The PR man took a deep breath. "Damn right we did," he said.
"We worked our tails off, talking to responsible people down in
Newburg County. People like the Jaycees and the Farm Bureau.
We built up a lot of support—"

"Exactly," the lawyer cut him short. "Things were looking
rosy for Buckeye. Murren was solidly behind you, and you were
getting support from the whole area. Okay, things have changed.
But they haven't changed for the worse."

The flush on Ireland's face subsided. "Go on," he said suspiciously.

The lawyer hid any triumph he felt. "As Doyle just told us, he
did first-rate spade work. A lot of respected civic groups were
pro-Buckeye—or straddling the fence. Now, what happens when
they hear about a bunch of radicals resorting to violence? Do
you think they're going to associate themselves with crazies?
Hell no! Times have changed. If you want to face facts, Davis
Quentin's murder was probably a big boost for Buckeye."

"Wait a minute," ordered Ireland. "You're leaving out some
pretty important people, aren't you?"

The lawyer was puzzled. "Who? Heisse—and the AEC? They
can't reverse themselves on your permit. And they don't have
any reason to. The FBI? You heard them, Sherry. They're dig-
ging in—"

"Not them," said Ireland curtly. "The crazies!"

"They're the last people in the world you have to worry
about!"

This legal serenity infuriated Sheridan Ireland. "You're
damned calm about a pack of hoods who don't stop at anything
—including murder—to get their way. They could be cooking
up something right now! What if they start putting bombs under
our powerlines? God knows they do it on the Coast!"

"Take it from me, you don't have to worry about anything like that," said the lawyer with a superior smile. "This isn't a gang of professional radicals. I've checked into the Carrs. He's a lawyer—"

"Some of those lawyers are the worst!"

"—and he's just like all the rest of the environmentalists—a respectable guy with a yen to lead a cause. Most PEP members are the same. I'm not saying they don't have a loony in the crowd. We've got pretty dramatic proof that they do. But right now most of them are scared stiff."

Sheridan Ireland wanted to believe him. "So you think they won't try anything else?"

The lawyer was positive. "If the Carrs have any sense at all, they're going to lie low and play dead."

* * *

The Carrs were the last to hear that Davis Quentin had been murdered, and they heard it the hard way.

Paul Carr got home from Woodruff & Jones at the usual time, forty-five minutes after Abby. Already, the aroma of a casserole permeated the kitchen. As usual he went straight to his wife, his jacket hooked from one finger over his shoulder, his briefcase tucked under the other arm, and kissed her. But there the routine collapsed. Instead of flinging down his belongings and heading for a tray of ice cubes, he sank into a chair, looking shell-shocked.

"What is it, honey?" Abby cried in alarm.

"I don't know how to tell you."

Instinctively Abby scanned the list of wifely anxieties. "Have you lost your job? You didn't have an accident, did you, Paul? Or Daddy—it isn't anything to do with him, is it? Are you sick . . . ?"

Possibility after possibility, and Paul did nothing but shake his head. Finally he rubbed a hand down his jaw hard enough to leave streaks of white. "No, nothing like that. It's that guy who was killed up in Murren."

"Murren?" Abby repeated blankly. "Oh, Murren." She had already turned the death of Inspector Quentin into one of those terrible things that happen. "For heaven's sake, you scared me.

Oh, it was a tragedy. And they shouldn't have thrown rocks. But it's over now, and we simply have to forget it."

"We can't. I guess you didn't hear the radio."

By now she was sitting at the table with him, clasping his hand. "I never hear it at the hospital. You know that."

"Quentin didn't just have an accident. The police say he was deliberately murdered."

She jerked back her hand as if it had been bitten. "That's impossible."

"I don't know the details," he continued dully, "but the police are certain. He . . . he was hit more than once."

Abby licked suddenly dry lips. "How can they tell? Probably he hit his head when he fell. That would look as if he'd been hit twice."

Wearily, Paul shook his head. "They don't make mistakes like that when they do autopsies, Abby."

"Everybody makes mistakes!" She rose and opened the refrigerator. "Honestly, Paul, you talk yourself into such states! What you need is a drink. Then we'll have dinner—"

"I haven't told you the worst yet," he said baldly. "Before I left the office, the FBI phoned. They've been called in to investigate. We're supposed to go down to their office for questioning tomorrow morning."

"Us?" Abby put a hand against the refrigerator to steady herself. "Why do they want to question us?"

"We were there," he said.

Like a sleepwalker, Abby prepared two glasses and brought them back to the table. "We weren't the only ones," she said suddenly. "What about everybody else who was out at Murren?"

"I don't know. I suppose they'll be talking to some of them."

"You suppose?" she cried. "It isn't fair for them to single us out! Why should we let them? I'll tell you what, Paul. Let's call everybody in PEP. Let's go to the FBI as a group!"

Carr buried his face in his glass, took a long swallow, then reached for a handful of nuts. In surprise, Abby watched him play for time.

"I've been thinking . . ." he said finally.

"Yes?"

"Well, everybody knows who belongs to PEP. We'd be better off going by ourselves."

"What do you mean by that?" she demanded, narrowing her eyes.

"It means I don't want to go as part of PEP," he said impatiently.

"Paul! Are you ashamed of—"

"I'm ashamed to be identified with a murderer," he burst out.

Her look of shock goaded him on. "For Christ's sake, Abby— stop and think! I don't want the newspapers saying I've been questioned by the FBI in connection with a killing. That kind of publicity is lethal. It could ruin my career. It already has ruined PEP!"

"PEP hasn't been ruined," she said fiercely.

"Face facts," he told her. "Somebody who went up to Murren with us deliberately killed a man."

"We don't know that," she shot back. "It could have been somebody who was already there. PEP went to Murren in good faith. Even if some lunatic trailed along with us, it isn't our fault."

Paul was harsh. "It doesn't make any difference whether it was our fault or not. It's what people think that counts."

They sat down to the casserole in unhappy silence. Finally, Abby took the plunge.

"You know, Paul," she said, "we could lose this whole fight by default. If we just keep quiet, everybody will look on us as a pack of homicidal maniacs—and Buckeye will be poisoning us before we know it."

Unresponsively he concentrated on his plate.

"That won't do your career much good, will it?"

She had touched a sensitive spot and he looked up quickly. Careful not to catch his eye, she continued, "Sneaking out of the Federal Building tomorrow morning with our tails between our legs is the worst thing we can do. Inspector Quentin's murder is bound to create a lot of publicity—at least locally. We should capitalize on it."

Paul toyed with his salad. "You may be right."

"I know I am! The only thing for us to do is to counterattack!"

CHAPTER 6

The Carrs were not the only ones overreacting to the FBI.

"Do you mean that the Feds are in there with Ben right now?" Tony Martinelli asked hoarsely.

"The folks back in Newburg won't like the sound of that," said Val Oakes, shaking his head.

Safford's secretary regarded the three representatives clustered around her desk with tolerance. "There's nothing to worry about," Madge Anderson assured them. "Remember that Mr. Safford was on the spot the night that AEC official was murdered. The FBI is just asking him if he noticed anything that might be a clue."

But a hard day in committee had not left the nation's legislators looking on the sunny side.

"That's the same story they hand out to every poor sap they grill," Tony said broodingly.

Even Elsie Hollenbach, who pushed a citizen's duty to cooperate with her government until she was the terror of half of Washington, was not encouraging.

"It is unfortunate that so many constituents equate police interrogation with police accusation," she declared. "We, of course, know better. But it would be wise to keep word of this interview from reaching Newburg."

"It would be best of all if Ben had never heard of this Murren place," said Tony.

"Oh, for heaven's sake!" Madge began just as the inner door opened.

Under the intent gaze of his colleagues, Ben Safford escorted a clean-cut young man to the corridor, shook his hand, and courteously said good-by. He was halfway back to his own quarters before he woke to the unnatural silence.

"Anything wrong?" he asked mildly.

"How did it go?" Tony asked tightly. "You didn't spill anything, did you?"

Safford blinked. "There wasn't much that I could tell them," he said, since everybody was interested. "I was inside the Grange for the whole riot, eating some godawful lemon cake. The minister went out and tried reasoning with the protesters. And I know that the guy from Lomax got as far as the porch. But I didn't see a thing."

"Good," said Tony.

He was the only one who saw law enforcement agencies as foes. Val and Elsie, consummate politicians both, knew the real enemy was the ingrained suspicion with which the American voter views his elected representative.

"It's a very great shame that you were there at all," said Elsie.

These were Ben's sentiments exactly. But fair is fair. "It was a greater shame for Davis Quentin," he said, automatically opening the cabinet and setting out glasses.

"And they're mad as wet hens about it over at the AEC," said Val Oakes, accepting his drink.

In Tony's world, personal loyalty ranked very high. "Sure they are," he said. "How would you feel if some nut started taking pot shots at Owen?"

But gunning down Congressman Oakes's administrative assistant was not a good parallel, as Val made clear. "No, it isn't that. Andy Heisse has been steaming around the Hill all morning, complaining to the committee. He wants to make sure that the FBI investigation doesn't turn into a hatchet job on the AEC."

Tony understood this, too. "Boy, these guys never learn, do they? Next thing we know, Heisse will be claiming executive privilege."

"I wonder where Lou is," said Ben hastily, keeping a weather eye on Elsie. Despite appearances, this was not a social gathering. L. Lamar Flecker (D., Ala.) and his subcommittee were wrestling with an amendment to the National Meteorological Services Bill.

Mrs. Hollenbach had settled herself gracefully in a chair, every lock of her iron-gray hair in place, her silk suit as fresh as it had been eight hours earlier. She transformed her corner of Ben's office into a tearoom of impeccable gentility. This might mislead the unwary, but not her fellow committee members.

Fortunately, she showed no disposition to sink her teeth into Tony, let alone the appropriation for a new weather ship off Newfoundland. Val Oakes had captured her attention.

"Andy Heisse," she said reminiscently.

"He's no worse than the rest of them," said Val obscurely.

Ben did not know if he was referring to the other AEC commissioners, or a broader field—but he did not propose to ask. Not with the Republican Party of California linking Heisse to Elsie, one way or another.

"He's an easy man to underestimate," she announced. "A lot of our people expected him to run for governor. But when the President offered him this appointment, he accepted immediately."

Tony was less delicate about California's recent Democratic landslide. "Not everybody can buck a trend the way you can, Elsie. Heisse'll go back and run when he thinks he's got an outside chance of winning."

Elsie, who could run on a laundry ticket in Marin County, came as near a pleased simper as was possible for her.

"Unless," Tony added, blasting peace and harmony, "unless Heisse is hiding skeletons in the closet over there at the AEC!"

"I have every confidence in Andrew Heisse's integrity and competence," said Elsie, endorsing a candidate so to speak. "Furthermore, the AEC is a widely respected agency, with high standards in a very sensitive area. It is well within Commissioner Heisse's province to deprecate any random intrusions into this difficult area. As for skeletons in the closet, as you put it—"

"Hold your horses, Elsie!" The shot across her bow came from Mrs. Hollenbach's fellow Republican. "You'd be surprised at what goes on over there. If they're uptight—well, they've got good reason to be. Poor Ben has already run into something the AEC doesn't like broadcasting to the world."

Poor Ben took Elsie's part. "You mean the murder, Val? As I understand it, this is the first time this has happened."

With a walrus flap of the hand, Val indicated that he did not mean murder. "This bunch you've got protesting over Buckeye. There's been a protest over every single plant—and some of them are still going on. Heisse and his buddies always troop up to the committee with a lot of sweet talk about partners-in-progress. They don't talk about the hundreds—thousands—of people who are dead set against them."

"The Joint Committee doesn't listen to the opposition much either," murmured Tony. Most critics of the AEC are not admirers of its congressional watchdog.

Val ignored this gibe. "Then, lately there's this sweat about who knows what—and when."

Seeing that he had lost them, he addressed himself to Ben. "I'll bet you'll find your protesters knew all about the application for Buckeye—long before the AEC authorized any public announcement. They came to the first hearings primed for bear!"

It had not occurred to Ben.

"Yup," said Val. "These days there's someone inside the AEC who's passing information. Not nuclear secrets or anything like that. Just enough to keep Andy Heisse hopping. Ordinarily, the AEC and a utility put together a scenario and expect to bull it through before the opposition can organize. But they can't do it now that these environment freaks have started infiltrating."

"Well, that explains why Heisse doesn't welcome the FBI with open arms," said Tony, conceding his error.

Elsie was caught. As the embodiment of rectitude, she deplored this cynicism. As a practicing politician, she knew there is only one sane way to handle dirty linen. She was still wavering when Lou Flecker came bustling in.

"Sorry to keep you all waiting. But the Speaker buttonholed me. He wants to tell you that he attaches the highest importance to putting a new weather reporting ship up there in the Atlantic."

"Have a drink, Lou," said Ben kindly.

But Val Oakes passed judgment anyway. "You know, the Speaker isn't the man he was. I think he got scared out of his wits when it looked as if he might have to be President. To tell you the truth, I don't think he's recovered to this day!"

*   *

Even with the FBI parading in and out of the AEC and Congressman Safford's office, the murder of Davis Quentin was not front-page news. In Washington, a bad joke by the Secretary of State outranks a GS-15, dead or alive, any day.

In Newburg, things were different, as Ben was to be reminded.

Elsie and Lou Flecker had already left when Madge entered with the pile of homework she assembled for him every evening. The stragglers were not even pretending to be working.

"I'll let you in on a little secret," Tony said, flashing a smile that included Madge in his confidence, "I don't even understand what an occluded cold front is—and I don't want to. All I want to know is whether I should wear a raincoat or not. Eighteen million bucks is a lot to spend for that."

Val had already put floating weather bureaus out of his mind. "Best be going," he said, without moving a muscle. "I'm giving out prizes at a convention of home economists tonight."

"How come nobody ever asks me to judge baking contests?"

"Good God!" Ben exclaimed.

"Hey, now wait a minute," said Tony, hurt.

But Ben had just come across the Newburg *News* in Madge's neat pile. One look was enough.

BUCKEYE PROTEST ENDS IN MURDER

AEC MAN VICIOUSLY SLAIN

STATE POLICE, FBI, INVESTIGATING MURREN HOMICIDE

"Boy, they sure went all out," said Tony, leaning over to study the biggest, blackest headlines he had seen in a long while.

"The *News* has more experience with zoning laws," Ben explained. "Besides, I expect this is the first murder in Murren since Gerry Kekkala found his wife with the County Commissioner."

Beneath the headlines were three photographs. One was Mrs. Lorraine Westerfeld with her mouth open. Another was a blurred shot of the Murren Grange Hall, behind police barriers. The third was an informal photo of Ben Safford.

". . . 'violence is no answer,' said Congressman Safford who was also present," Ben read aloud. "'This nation has no foreign foe half as dangerous . . .'"

"Did you say that?" Tony was awed.

"I did not," said Ben. "Janet must have issued a statement when Henry Hough asked for one. I guess she was in a hurry."

"Now, now," said Val, lumbering to his feet. "I don't like to hear you sounding ungrateful, Ben. Just think how it would look if that paper told everybody all about the murder, told everybody you were Johnny-on-the-spot, then ended up saying you weren't available for comment."

But Ben was still reading. The Newburg *News* had been electrified by the sheer drama of it all.

". . . eyewitnesses describe threats from Paul Carr and other PEP members. Carr, a local attorney, denies making such threats. 'I was exercising my constitutional right of free speech,' he told our reporter this morning outside the Federal Building where he was 'co-operating' with the FBI investigation. Special Agent-in-Charge James Fitton declines comment . . ."

Ben whistled.

"Laying it on good and strong, aren't they?" Val commented. "Well, that means one thing sure as shooting. You're in for a lot more fun down your way. Just be careful to stay on the side of the angels, Ben. Speaking of which, I'd better get going or all those cooking teachers will die of lonesomeness."

Tony lingered long enough to add his own brand of folk wisdom. "If it was me, Ben, I'd find a lot of things to do in Washington."

This was good advice. But, as events were to prove, not good enough.

* *

Tonight the casserole was getting cold.

Abby Carr read and reread the Newburg *News* until she knew it by heart. ". . . outsiders trying to intimidate Murren voters. Despite these efforts, the referendum will be held as scheduled. Leading Buckeye proponent George Barry, who found Davis Quentin's body, says, 'We're not letting them scare us' . . . Oh, Paul!"

Paul Carr had read the Newburg *News* at breakfast, and not since. In a trance, he had gone to work, where his expression effectively rebuffed everybody. Everybody, that is, but the elderly Mr. Woodruff. At three o'clock in the afternoon he had come into Paul's office and, with considerable embarrassment, suggested a few days off—"until things blow over."

"I'm not going to let them get away with it," Paul said, breaking a long silence.

Abby caught her breath. "That's right! Just like we were saying last night! We've got to fight back! The Newburg *News* is a joke—"

This could have been a robin chirping as far as Paul was concerned. He was talking to himself. "Unless I do something, I'm going to be crucified. They're already nervous as cats downtown at the firm . . ."

Abby's hand went to her throat in distress.

". . . and then what? I couldn't get elected dog catcher!"

The cold monotone frightened her.

"And they'll ram through Buckeye," she said timidly. "That's what they're trying to do, Paul. Why, maybe that's why Quentin was killed! Have you ever thought of that?"

Unseeingly, he looked at her across the kitchen table. Then, to her relief, he smiled. "It could be, honey. It could be. But anyway, I've been thinking about what we can do. And I checked a couple of law books."

"Yes?" She was almost afraid to ask.

"What we're going to do," said Paul Carr, "is sue the Newburg *News* for libel."

CHAPTER 7

The Newburg *News* circulated more widely than Tony Martinelli would have believed. For example, Tristate Electric had a couple of subscriptions. Bored clerks routinely clipped stories about downed wires, billing errors and linemen rescuing kittens from trees. With Buckeye Atomic in the air, executive readership began picking up. PR was regularly monitoring "Letters to the Editor," and even ghostwriting some.

Now, for the first time, the Newburg *News* reached the president's desk. Sheridan Ireland liked the editorial he was reading.

". . . so-called environmentalists. But Mr. Carr and his PEP sympathizers don't mind filling the environment with flying rocks. Murren taxpayers have their interests, too. But did they run agitators out of town? Did they . . . ? That's telling them!"

The lawyer was more discerning. "Tristate takes a lot of advertising in the Newburg *News*, doesn't it?"

Ireland's underlip jutted stubbornly. "What of it? Carr and the rest of those clowns have bought a lot of space—here, look at this!"

He rattled the offending page.

IMPORTANT PEP MEETING TUESDAY NIGHT

28 Clinton Road
Lincolnwood

For further information call: Joan Libby 375-7567

Steve Fels 777-9853

If Ireland really wanted to equate this amateurish insert with Tristate's agency-prepared ads, the lawyer was not going to fight.

"I've got a good mind to call up the editor and congratulate him," Ireland said. "If more newspapers had the guts, or the gumption—"

"Don't!" said the lawyer tersely. "I have a hunch the Newburg *News* may have gone a little too far. After all, Carr is a lawyer."

"Godamned troublemaker!"

"And don't you forget it," said the lawyer, rising to go. "The last thing Buckeye needs before the referendum is more trouble. Keep your hands off Murren, Sherry!"

No rugged individualist could accept advice like this. But Sheridan Ireland was not as unreconstructed as he liked to pretend. Tristate always preached the old-time religion of hard work, frugality and independence. But it also retained an advertising agency in Chicago and lobbyists in Columbus and Washington. Sheridan Ireland did not pay a lawyer good money to ignore him completely.

So he did not call Henry Hough, editor of the Newburg *News.* Instead he called Mrs. Lorraine Westerfeld.

Since Ireland had forgotten about her Texaco station, the background noises that clanged over the line, as well as intermittent bells, puzzled him at first.

"Well, my goodness!" exclaimed Lorraine. "I didn't hear what the girl said—Joe, take care of the pump . . . Mr. Ireland?"

Flattered and flustered, thought Ireland indulgently. He swiveled his chair around to survey downtown Cincinnati, not his own luxurious office, while he spoke.

"I just wanted to be sure you good people in Murren are getting along all right in spite of your excitement." Ireland had a special voice for nice little women.

"It's not a lot of fun," said this one, jolting him.

"I've just been reading the Newburg *News.*"

Exasperation crackled across the miles. "Everybody's reading the Newburg *News,*" said Lorraine. If she was thrilled to be talking to the president of Tristate, she was hiding it. "I don't know what got into Henry. God knows, the murder was bad enough!"

Frowning, Ireland swung back to his desk. "I thought he did a first-rate job. It's time somebody exposed the Carrs and the rest of them for what they are. Maybe we should order some reprints of that editorial."

Now Lorraine was downright peevish. "I guess you haven't heard."

"Heard what?"

"The Carrs are suing the Newburg *News* for libel."

Unfortunately, Ireland said the first thing that came into his head. "I don't know why you should sound that way, Mrs. Westerfeld. A libel suit may be a problem for the Newburg *News*. But I don't see why it should hurt us. In fact, it may help swing support for the referendum."

She counted up to ten. Then: "None of this is doing any of *us* a lot of good."

Being no fool, Ireland realized they were not talking about the same *us*. Alarmed, he said, "You're still in Buckeye's corner, aren't you?"

"Sure I am," said Lorraine. "And most other people around here are, too. But it's like I was telling George Barry. By the time you've got the police coming back again and again, and people accusing each other of murder—well, it's pretty damned hard to feel enthusiastic about anything, including Buckeye!"

"We're going to have to do something about that," said Ireland.

"If you can!"

"Believe me, Mrs. Westerfeld," he said emphatically, "I not only can, but will! We're not letting anything stop Buckeye at this late date—nothing at all!"

*   *

At the main entrance to the AEC headquarters building the guard was unyielding.

"Sure I know you, Mr. Gladstone," he said, meanwhile checking off the names of incoming secretaries. "I know you've got a pass, too. But I've got to see it."

Clumsy with frustration, Gladstone pawed through his briefcase. "Dammit, it's here somewhere . . ."

Having seen this scene re-enacted a hundred times, the guard was unmoved as Gladstone grew more and more exasperated, until, "Here! Here it is."

He was thrusting the security badge at the guard's nose when Jim Vorhees came up behind him.

"Hi, Roger. Having trouble?"

Gladstone was reassembling his belongings. "I've got so many clearances to so many top-secret places all over the damn country that I can't keep them straight. Well, I'm inside, that's what counts. It'd be a helluva thing if I kept the commissioner waiting because I couldn't find my pass."

"Commissioner Heisse?" Vorhees asked.

Gladstone shot him a quick look. "Yes, I've got an appointment with him."

"I'll bet the girls were trying to get hold of you all morning," said Vorhees regretfully, leading the way to an elevator. "Andy's had to go over to the White House. But why don't you come along to my office and see if there's any way I can help."

It was smooth as silk, but Roger Gladstone had had enough dealings with the AEC to read between the lines.

"Fine," he said equably. "I always know I've got a pipeline to Heisse when I talk to you, Jim. And I can get down to brass tacks a little sooner. I'm worried about Buckeye."

"So are we," Vorhees said.

"I can tell," Gladstone replied with a grin. "Is he really over at the White House, Jim?"

Vorhees was unruffled. "He's not in his office anyway. We got four calls from Ireland yesterday . . . here's my office . . . take a chair . . . Where was I? . . . Oh, yes, Ireland. We got a lot of calls from him—and that sent Andy hightailing out of here."

Totally serious, Gladstone said, "Look Jim, I've got Ireland on my neck too. That's what sent me over here. I've got a feeling I'm getting out of my depth." He stopped, then asked a blunt question. "The AEC isn't getting cold feet about Buckeye, is it? Because of Davis Quentin, or anything else?"

Vorhees dropped the pen he had been fiddling with. "What makes you think that?"

Shrugging, Gladstone said, "I just want to be sure. I'm a simple guy, Jim. Ireland wants to build Buckeye. Lomax wants to sell him a generator. The AEC has already given us the permit. I thought that put us all on the same side."

"*If,*" Vorhees interjected neatly, "if the people in Murren vote the way they should."

"That's no problem," Gladstone said. "It's just up to us to make sure that they do. But what I've been wondering—"

"The AEC co-operates with informing the public, Roger," said Vorhees sternly. "But we're very careful about laying ourselves open to any charge of interfering with . . . oh, hello, Nina. Didn't see you there. Come on in. Do you know Roger Gladstone here? He's from Lomax Tool."

"Buckeye," she said with a ravishing smile at Gladstone. "We're being especially careful about that, Mr. Gladstone. Paul Carr seems to be boiling to sue everybody in sight."

Roger Gladstone was the only one who had not read the Newburg *News.*

*   *

Commissioner Heisse was not at the White House. He was in the New House Office Building.

"So I said—Andy, why tell me? Come along and tell Ben yourself." Val Oakes could not have been more genial to voters from South Dakota.

"I'd appreciate a minute if you've got it," said Heisse. He was almost excessively respectful to Congressman Safford, which stamped him as a hardened operator.

Ben could scarcely refuse although he was already running late for the afternoon. "Come on in . . ."

"Not me," said Val. "I've got to go read up on rain-making dances. I figure two hired Indians from back home might save the country a whole bushel of money."

With a massive wink at Ben, he glided away.

Heisse, to his credit, did not waste any part of this courtesy call on idle courtesies.

"I was telling Mr. Oakes that we're worried about Buckeye Atomic over at the AEC."

"The murder?" Ben hoped he was not going to be asked to take on the FBI.

"That was a kick in the belly," said Heisse. "But we've got it under control now. Davis Quentin was just an ordinary hard-working stiff. He didn't even have any information about

Buckeye. All they found in his papers—here and in Murren—
were his usual reports. No, it looks as if the killer made a big mistake. He was aiming at someone else."

"That's probably keeping everybody in Murren happy," said
Ben caustically.

Heisse nodded. "Murren and Newburg are what's worrying
me, Mr. Congressman. When the AEC licenses a power plant—
well, we're used to a lot of flack."

"You should be," said Ben.

Unoffended, Heisse said, "You name 'em—we've had 'em. But
we still don't like blood in the streets."

When Ben did not applaud, Heisse hitched himself forward.
"And we don't want to be involved in a snow job, either. If the
people of Murren don't want Buckeye—why, they shouldn't
have it foisted on them. That's our position."

All this virtue left Ben cold. "Sure," he said.

"Now the AEC people who follow these developments agreed
with Tristate's forecast. Until last weekend Murren was all for
Buckeye. The referendum was in the bag."

The politics of California must be as strange as everybody said,
Ben thought. Aloud he asked, "Does the AEC take secret polls?"

This was not treated as a joke.

"At times, we have used them," said Heisse ponderously. "But
not recently."

"No, of course not."

"And despite Quentin's murder—"

"—and Paul Carr's libel suit?" Ben was beginning to enjoy
himself.

"That's right," Heisse agreed. "Despite everything, we at the
AEC understood that popular opinion in general—and in Murren
in particular—was pro-Buckeye."

When he paused inquiringly, Ben had to give him what he had
come for. "That's how I hear it, too," he said.

"Then why is Sheridan Ireland calling me up to tell me that
we've got to make an all-out, last-minute push?"

Ben did not know.

"And what does he expect us to do?"

Ben did not know that one either.

"I'll level with you, Mr. Safford. Ireland worries me. Most of the businessmen we deal with have plenty of horse sense. But Ireland—well, he's different."

Defending Sheridan Ireland was somebody else's job. "You granted him a license to build Buckeye Atomic," Ben retorted.

Heisse reared back. "Don't misinterpret me! Buckeye Atomic is going to be a model installation. Tristate's technical people are topnotch! And Lomax Tool, especially Gladstone, are as good as they come. Buckeye exceeds all the AEC's minimum standards. And it's going to be a soundly financed operation, too. We're completely satisfied with the whole package. It's not Buckeye— it's Ireland, the man. To be honest with you, I don't trust his judgment."

"His judgment can't be all bad," Ben murmured, but Heisse did not hear him.

"I just want you to know that the AEC takes its responsibility for public safety and public self-determination very seriously, Mr. Safford."

Translated, this meant that the AEC—or Commissioner Heisse —was scared to death Ireland was going to kick up a stink.

"But what do you think he's going to do?" Ben asked.

"I was hoping you could tell me," Heisse said frankly. "Ireland arranged that voter's night in Murren—and we all remember what happened there."

Ben knew better than to treat this as a serious accusation. In the time-honored tradition of the practicing politician, Heisse was simply trying to keep his distance from dirt.

"The AEC is willing to wait until the people of Murren make their will known," he said with a man-to-man smile. "Until then, we intend that the issue of Buckeye be as low-keyed and non-controversial as possible. What we'd like to see is a breathing space, where your people can decide about Buckeye on its merits."

Ben could decipher this one, too. But he was not making any announcements about Buckeye to Andrew Heisse or anybody else.

"That sounds pretty sensible to me," he said, as Murren's elected representative. "But I'd better warn you—"

Heisse tensed.

"—from what I read and hear, it sounds too good to be true."

CHAPTER 8

The storm clouds appeared that evening when Janet called.

"Ben, you'll never guess what's come up!" she began without preliminaries.

"I'm afraid to," he said. "Don't tell me that somebody's fire-bombed Lorraine's filling station?"

An audible cluck told him that was not funny. "And things do seem to be calming down, thank God!"

"Do you mean PEP is lying low?"

No, that was not what Janet meant. Activists were still handing out petitions on the streets of downtown Newburg and ringing doorbells in Murren. "But they're mostly students. The grownups seem to have cooled off."

"There's nothing like murder to shake even hard-core do-gooders," Ben commented.

"Don't be silly," Janet told him bracingly. "What worries the Lincolnwood crowd is how much the lawsuit will cost. Apparently there's been a lot of criticism of Paul Carr for going ahead on his own, without consulting anybody else."

"You mean to tell me that Carr didn't consult his supporters?" Ben asked.

Janet didn't think so. "But that's not why I called. Ben, you know I'm president of the Women's Alliance this year?"

Since she was always president of something or other, Ben had forgotten.

"Well, this afternoon I got a telephone call—from Sheridan Ireland's office, no less. Would I, on behalf of the Woman's Alliance, care to participate in an all-expense-paid trip to Washington? For a three-day colloquium on the peacetime potential of the atom?"

Ben, who had been braced for some new wrinkle in the Equal Rights Amendment, sat up.

"I thought you'd be interested," said Janet with a chuckle.

"I am," said Ben. "What can you tell me about this so-called colloquium?"

"Just about everything," said Janet, without false modesty.

After prolonged thought, Tristate Electric had decided on its eleventh-hour stratagem to guarantee a whopping pro-Buckeye vote in the upcoming Murren referendum. This was a three-day bash, disguised as a study session. Mrs. Westerfeld, Emily Coughlin, Reverend Baines, and "everybody who's anybody in Murren" as Janet phrased it, were going to be wined and dined.

"There are laws against buying votes," Ben observed.

"That's where I come in," Janet said. "After all, I'm not going to vote in the referendum."

The rest of Sheridan Ireland's window dressing consisted of Mayor Wilhelm of Newburg, Fritz Toomey, talkmaster on WNBG and other local luminaries.

"About as subtle as a concrete mixer," Ben was saying when another thought struck him. "The peacetime potential of the atom? Does that mean the AEC is sponsoring this junket?"

It had been very carefully worded, Janet reported. "The AEC would be 'co-operating' in some of the technical presentations."

"Of course, they can't duck entirely," said Ben, recalling Heisse. "Their permit to Buckeye sticks them with Ireland, whether they like it or not. Still, I'll bet there was plenty of arm twisting."

"Mr. Ireland wouldn't take no for an answer from me," said Janet complacently.

"Oh, you're coming, are you?" Ben belatedly asked.

"I sure am," said Janet. "I've got a lot of shopping to do. You know how I love Garfinkel's. Save Tuesday lunch for me, will you?"

Ben made a note of it, then asked if Tristate was inviting the opposition.

Janet had not seen the complete guest list. "But I doubt it," she said. "Would you invite Paul Carr—after all that's happened?"

*   *

Neither would Sheridan Ireland.

"But he's in for a big surprise," said Paul Carr, cupping a hand around the mouthpiece. "Look, are you sure you can get hold of an invitation for me? I don't want to have to fight my way in."

Outside his study, the vacuum cleaner was humming closer. Saturday morning was an awkward time to try lining things up, but it was the only time Carr had.

"Good," he said. "Then I can show them—"

A sudden roar drowned him out.

"Oh, I'm sorry!" Abby apologized. "I didn't know you were on the phone."

"Listen, I've got to go," said Paul, the moment the door shut behind her. "I'll call you as soon as I get to Washington. No, maybe it would be better if you called me. I'll be staying at the Mayflower."

Abby switched off when Paul came sauntering out. "Who was that?" she asked.

"Bob Greene," he replied nonchalantly. "I just want to be sure he's got everything under control here while I'm in Washington making sure that Ireland doesn't pull a fast one."

Abby was still of two minds about Paul's plans.

"Stop worrying, honey," he said, affectionately reaching out to tousle her hair. "I'm just reminding them that we are watching what they do."

Seeing she was still unconvinced, he added, "Look, we don't want to let them steal the referendum, do we?"

"No-o."

Paul was about to go back to his desk when she spoke again.

"Paul"—and the thoughtful inflection made him stiffen—"Paul, I've been thinking. Do you think I should write to Daddy?"

Relief invaded him. "Sure, if you want to," he said carelessly.

Pleased to be making a contribution, Abby rushed off to the desk. In her eagerness, she completely forgot what Liz Greene had told her yesterday.

The Greenes, including Bob, were going up to Chicago for a long weekend.

*   *

Ben's invitation arrived two days later, hand-carried by private messenger.

". . . dinner at the Shoreham, to meet with Tristate's guests from Newburg County," Ben read aloud, skipping the rest of the text to fasten on the signature. " 'Sheridan Ireland!' I suppose he thinks I can't resist any chance to get a crack at a bunch of voters."

Madge had already asked around. "The whole Ohio delegation has been invited," she reported.

By now, Ben was beginning to take Ireland's measure. "That's just to prove this isn't a sneak play. I'll bet he's scheduled a prayer breakfast, too—complete with Billy Graham." He went back to doublecheck his reading. "That's what I thought. Not a word about the AEC. Well, Madge. I don't think there's any problem."

"A previous engagement?" she said brightly.

"How did you guess?"

"Mrs. Lundgren is attending, isn't she?"

Otherwise, of course, Ben would be forced to turn out. Because, for the officeholder, keeping tabs beats a declaration of conscience any day of the week.

*   *

Ben was not the only absent friend at the Shoreham on Wednesday.

"Commissioner Heisse was sorry to miss you all," said Jim Vorhees, deliberating over a platter of canapes. "But he had to go out to the Coast."

Despite pressing invitations, Vorhees was the only senior AEC official present.

With a prominent, civic-minded Newburg matron beside him, Sheridan Ireland had to watch his step. "Too bad," he said sourly. Then, remembering he was a host, he turned to Janet, "And we're sorry Congressman Safford couldn't make it, Mrs. Lundgren."

"Well, I see Senator Cruft," she consoled him. "And he may know something about atomic energy. He certainly doesn't know anything about Newburg County."

This earned her an amused but wary look from Vorhees. Ireland, however, was already gravitating toward his other guests.

They were enjoying themselves. In fact, they were enjoying themselves so thoroughly that it was hard to sustain the pretense that this was anything other than a party.

Still one Tristate staffman was doing his best. "Our after-dinner speaker is going to be Dr. Edmund Fellner, from the University of Maryland," he informed Lorraine Westerfeld.

Gone were the shabby sweater and dungarees that Lorraine wore at the pumps. She was as sedate as Janet in a soft suit and a blouse with frilly edging at the throat. Her short gray hair had been transformed into a blue-white cap. But when she opened her mouth, it was the same old Lorraine.

"No wonder utility rates are so high," she said, exchanging her empty glass for a fresh martini from the white-jacketed waiter. "I wonder how much this is costing Tristate."

Reverend Baines pursed his lips. "Dr. Fellner? That should be instructive. He was featured in *Time*, wasn't he?"

Others were more candid. "Yes sirree, the champagne flowed like water." Mayor Wilhelm was going strong as he and Roger Gladstone approached. "Hello there, girls. I was just telling Mr. . . . Mr. . . ."

"Gladstone. Call me Roger," he supplied before nodding at the others.

"I was just telling Roger here that Ireland really knows how to lay it on," Wilhelm continued robustly. "Flying the whole bunch of us up here in the company plane! Hell, it's worth listening to a speech or two!"

Janet, and to a lesser extent Lorraine, were accustomed to Mayor Wilhelm, who took shameless advantage of his eighty-odd years. Vorhees and Roger Gladstone both suspected the champagne.

Out of the hum of convivial conversation and clinking of glassware came another earnest voice, "Then, after lunch at Harvey's tomorrow, we will be taking our guests out to AEC headquarters for a movie, entitled *Atoms In the Service of Mankind*. Then, we'll be coming back here for a question-and-answer period. Then, during the social hour . . ."

"God help them!"

"Val," Janet exclaimed with pleasure.

Congressman Oakes emerged from the crowd and, without en-

dangering a drop of his Bourbon, bussed Janet with the heartiness of an old friend.

"Nobody'd ever believe a man as homely as Ben could have a
sister who looked like you," he said.

This put Mayor Wilhelm on his mettle. "Yup," he said with an
elderly leer. "We're going to have to do a little stepping out.
What Fred doesn't know won't hurt him."

Janet laughed and completed a round of introductions. But Val
had recognized a kindred spirit. "Your Honor, you won't get any
chance to step off the rails. The way I hear it, they're going to
keep your nose to the grindstone."

"Young fella," said Mayor Wilhelm, "I didn't come all this
way to miss Ninth Street!"

Lorraine was right there with him. "And I want to go shopping in Georgetown."

"That's right," Emily Coughlin twittered. "Say what you
want, there's no real selection in Newburg."

"Now, I don't like to hear you ladies say that," said the mayor.

Janet, meanwhile, had been left with Val.

"Ben not here?" he asked, looking around with sleepy curiosity.

"He couldn't make it," said Janet.

"Umph," said Val Oakes. His views on free drinks were well
known. But he also realized that there were times when it was
wise for a congressman to make himself scarce. "And, of course,
it's a big help having a sister like you," he told Janet elliptically.
"I've always regretted being an only child."

"Congressman Oakes," Jim Vorhees explained to Gladstone,
"is on the Joint Atomic Energy Committee."

"Oh, yes."

"You must have testified before us," said Val, when he learned
who Gladstone was. "Everybody else has. Jim here is up on the
Hill every other day."

"It just seems that way," said Vorhees with a pleasant smile.
"Excuse me . . ."

But he was back in seconds, breaking unceremoniously into
one of Val's celebrated anecdotes.

"Do you know who's over there in the corner?" he demanded.

"Paul Carr, that's who! Do you suppose that damned fool Ireland was stupid enough to ask him to this clambake?"

Janet and Val Oakes were practiced enough to ignore this glaring indiscretion.

"No, of course he didn't," said Gladstone warningly.

"Then how did he get in?" Vorhees lost his composure. "There are people at the door, you know!"

"What difference does it make?" Gladstone tried to cut him short.

With exemplary tact, Val took Janet by the arm. "Come on over and protect me while I talk to Senator Cruft. . . . . What's the trouble with this Paul Carr?"

In a sentence, Janet identified him.

"Oh, that one," said Val who forgot very little. "I suppose I can understand why he makes the boys nervous. But it's kind of strange, isn't it? The AEC isn't het up about Buckeye, the way Ireland is. But it's Vorhees who recognizes Carr, and Vorhees who sets up a yell . . ."

This was the very point that Jim Vorhees was shrugging off. "I've seen him somewhere, I guess. Or I saw a picture of him, when the FBI was questioning us about Davis Quentin. I recognized him—that's all. And I want to know what he's doing here and what we should do about it."

Gladstone studied him. "What can we do about it, but sit tight?"

With an effort at self-control, Vorhees said, "I'm warning you, Roger. Any more trouble about Buckeye, and the AEC is going to jerk your permit!"

"You can't!"

"Oh, can't we? Why do you think Heisse and the rest from the AEC didn't show up? Because the AEC isn't sticking its neck out—for you or Ireland. We've got enough on our hands without getting involved in murders!"

A melodious gong sounded through the smoky, crowded room. "We're ready to go inside, folks," an unseen Ireland could be heard bellowing jovially.

"Tell that to Paul Carr—not me," said Roger Gladstone, turning on his heel.

*   *

Dinner, as Janet, Lorraine, Mayor Wilhelm, and a lot of other independent witnesses agreed, did not go according to Sheridan Ireland's plan.

There was a magnificent floral centerpiece at the head table. There were charming bud vases at the more intimate tables for six that dotted the Shoreham's Blue Room.

But at one of these tables sat Paul Carr. Awareness of his presence seeped through the room, spreading uneasiness and expectation.

"I'm sorry," Jim Vorhees wrenched himself away from a long inspection of Table Eight, "I'm afraid I missed what you were saying, Mrs. Lundgren."

Janet had no intention of repeating her commonplace about Washington's spring weather, so she smiled encouragingly. Vorhees was not the first man to find her easy to confide in.

"We were afraid it was a mistake to draw attention to Buckeye again," he said in a low voice. "The best thing would have been to sit tight until after the referendum."

Across the table, Val Oakes had overheard. "You afraid Carr is going to start throwing rocks right here at the Shoreham?"

"Certainly not, Mr. Congressman," Vorhees said. "Or, at least, I hope not. But a good deal of time—"

"—and money!" Val interjected.

"—and money," Vorhees accepted this in good grace, "has been spent on Buckeye already. I hate to see someone like Carr wreck it."

At a neighboring table, throwing rocks was not in issue.

"I'd like to punch that guy in the nose," said Roger Gladstone, glowering in Paul Carr's direction.

Lorraine clamped a strong hand on his forearm. "Just simmer down and ignore him. That's the best way to deal with him."

"Absolutely," said Reverend Baines hastily. "The last thing we want is any repetition of what happened in Murren. That is . . . I mean . . ."

Gladstone ignored this welter of broken sentences, but he was not tasting much of the excellent roast beef. "He's got no business being here," he muttered, mouth full.

"He didn't have any business in Murren either," Lorraine pointed out. "And a whole lot of good that did us."

"In retrospect," said Baines, still trying to draw an inoffensive moral, "we all regret the idea of voter's night, excellent notion though it appeared at the time, Mrs. Westerfeld."

"Sure," said Lorraine gruffly, with a side look at Gladstone.

"If Sheridan would just keep hands off," said Gladstone, "we might get Buckeye built. Any more brilliant ideas are going to kill us."

"What I do not understand," Reverend Baines persisted, "is why Mr. Carr was invited. Surely he has made his opposition to Buckeye clear."

"That," said Gladstone, with a baleful look at Table Eight, "is the sixty-four thousand dollar question!"

Incredibly enough, the ripples caused by Paul Carr's presence did not reach the head table. Not that Sheridan Ireland was altogether content. There was, for instance, the AEC. Andy Heisse was into Buckeye as deeply as Tristate, the way Ireland saw it. But those gutless wonders over there were pussyfooting now that the pressure was on.

"If you ask me," said Mayor Wilhelm, speaking across Mrs. Bondurant of the PTA, "you're just throwing away good money. Murren's all set to give you a whopping approval!"

"I surely hope so," said Ireland, with a special twinkle for the PTA. "But we just want to be sure our good friends don't have any unanswered questions. Besides, Buckeye has caused some unpleasantness. We just wish to remind folks that it means a lot of good things, too."

"You can say that again," said the PTA fervently.

Reveling Murren voters, bigwigs like Senator Cruft, and his own share of cocktails and wine—all these kept Ireland from dwelling on grievances.

When he rose to speak, he was almost happy.

"Welcome to our colloquium on the peacetime uses of atomic energy, friends. Friends, I hope I can say, of Buckeye Atomic, which is going—"

"Mr. Ireland!"

The voice came from beyond Ireland's field of vision. While he fumbled in his breast pocket for his glasses, Paul Carr continued,

"I want to put you on notice. You have friends of Buckeye Atomic here. But you also have opponents."

Carr was twisting a napkin as he spoke but only his tablemates could see that. From the head table, he looked alarmingly resolute.

Ireland goggled at him, his mouth opening and closing spasmodically.

Carr was still speaking. "I know you, and your guests from Murren, wouldn't want to create the impression that both sides of this issue aren't being given a fair hearing."

The thin edge of defiance in his voice produced a groan in many throats.

"What did you . . ." Ireland sputtered incoherently. "How did you . . . ?"

"I know I'm no match for Tristate, and the AEC," Carr continued somberly. "But I'm going to try to remind all of us of the other side of this argument, if you'll allow me to."

There was a long silence. Then a few people clapped half-heartedly.

"Smart," said Val Oakes.

"It's a hard thing to refuse," Janet commented, turning to find her neighbor gone. Jim Vorhees was at the head table, talking to Sheridan Ireland with urgency.

Folding his arms, Paul Carr simply waited.

Sheridan Ireland sounded strangled. "Welcome aboard, Mr. Carr," he said, with a death's-head smile. "As I was saying, I think I can assure all of you that Dr. Edmund Fellner has an important message . . ."

Before Dr. Fellner got up to speak there was a hush into which two comments dropped like rocks, foreshadowing what was to come.

"This scientist for hire," said Paul Carr, without bothering to lower his voice.

And Sheridan Ireland didn't care who heard him either. "I just want someone to tell me how that SOB got in here!"

CHAPTER 9

Prayer breakfasts are not the only occupational hazard facing congressmen. Lunch in the House dining room, with visitors, from home, is another. Ben Safford had spent more hours than he liked discussing the famous bean soup.

"Besides," he told his companions, "I don't even like the stuff."

"It's very good," said Lorraine Westerfeld loyally. "But to tell you the truth, I've eaten enough food in the last three days" —she patted her midriff ruefully—"to last me for a week."

"So I hear," said Ben. "Ireland must think the way to Buckeye is through Murren's stomach."

Janet, who was pecking at her own lunch, flashed him an infinitesimal warning. Lorraine was a comfortable woman, but she was one of Buckeye's strongest supporters. It wouldn't do for Ben to forget this.

But lavish breakfasts, luncheons, dinners—and unlimited liquor —were not, it appeared, off bounds.

"I'll take a hamburger any day," Lorraine said. "Say, isn't that Elizabeth Bettman? My God, she's just a kid! And will you look at the hat on that other one!"

The winds of change had washed a new look into Congress. The leadership and most committee chairmen were tolerant in public, but Ben had heard denunciations of turtlenecks, hair transplants and attendance records that could not be repeated in polite company.

But there was an undeniable plus to these newcomers, and he was going to bring it up the next time the Majority Leader started repining. The House, whether you viewed it from the

Gallery or the restaurant, was a lot more colorful than it used to be.

Even Janet was not too blasé to ogle. "That's Bjorner, from Wisconsin. He's the one who wrote the book about his first term in Congress—and his divorce!"

Both ladies turned to Ben with undisguised reproach. He grinned unrepentantly. Glamor had never been his forte—if that was what you called exposing your colleagues and deserting your wife—and he was still getting re-elected.

"And there's Mr. Oakes!" Lorraine exclaimed. "I met him the other night. You know he was there at the dinner, Ben?"

Ben knew, all right. He had already heard Val's sardonic description of Paul Carr's gate-crashing act. But, mindful of Janet, he refrained from comment.

Lorraine said it for him. "You know, in a way you've got to hand it to Carr. He barged in and took over as if he didn't have a nerve in his body."

"I thought he was keyed up," said Janet reflectively. "Oh, I know he put a good face on it, but you could see he was under tremendous strain."

These differing views might be attributed to bias, or its absence. But both Lorraine and Janet had certainly had ample opportunity to make up their minds.

Because Paul Carr had not disappeared after dinner at the Shoreham. On the contrary, he had attached himself to the Newsburg party, joining their outings, attending (as many of the bona fide guests did not) all lectures and study sessions. He had asked probing questions. He had made one short speech.

"And even when he just sat there, everybody was aware of him, if you know what I mean," Janet described the tactics.

"The ghost at the feast," Ben said.

"A pain in the neck," Lorraine corrected him. "I don't understand why they didn't just throw him out. After all, everybody knew he wasn't invited. There he was anyway—lapping up the booze just like everybody else."

"He skipped the second dinner," Janet said.

"So did Mae Winter," said Lorraine. "And she says she saw Carr with a woman who was definitely not his wife."

"Lorraine!" Janet said disapprovingly.

Mrs. Westerfeld flushed. "Well, that's what Mae said. Not that it's anybody's business what Carr does in Washington, when he isn't bugging us. I still don't see why Ireland let him stay."

Ben associated Lorraine with frankness, not bitchiness, and he was glad to see her revert to it. At the same time, he was surprised. The leader of Murren's pro-Buckeye forces did not seem to know what had been going on in the inner circles.

"Ireland didn't want to," Ben reported. "The AEC and Gladstone got to him and talked sense."

"Sense?" Lorraine said pugnaciously.

"Absolutely," said Ben. He had Val's word for it, too. "In the first place, everybody wanted to avoid any semblance of physical force. That would have been playing right into Carr's hands."

"I suppose so," said Lorraine reluctantly.

"Oh come on, Lorraine. Would a news picture of Carr being hustled out of this meeting do Buckeye any good?" Ben did not wait for an answer. "And Carr's presence did take the AEC off the hook. Now they can say this really was a legitimate colloquium—not a payoff!"

This made her flare up again. "You mean all that talk about bribery? That's silly, and you know it. We're all Buckeye—and we have been from the beginning. Sure, people took advantage of this little trip to Washington. Who wouldn't? But you can't claim this is corruption! That's foolish. The only people who could say that—"

"—are young and probably ignorant," Ben finished swiftly. "But they're pretty damned intolerant these days, Lorraine. They think they've got a monopoly on virtue and morality, and they're conditioned to think the worst of anybody else. Sure, I know you were all having fun. But Paul Carr and his friends don't think that way."

She was genuinely indignant.

"Washington isn't the only place where Watergate made a difference," he said, ramming it home.

Janet never undercut Ben. She waited long enough for the air to clear, then said briskly, "Well, I always enjoy Washington, but I'm glad to be going home this afternoon."

"Me, too," said Lorraine bleakly. Then, giving Ben a no-hard-feelings smile, she said, "I've got a lot to do. The referendum's day after tomorrow, after all."

"I wish you luck," Ben said in the same spirit. "But I don't think you need it. From what I hear, Buckeye is going to win by a landslide."

She was pleased and showed it. "It sure is. But, we're not going to treat it like a sure thing until the last vote is counted."

*   *

Neither was the opposition, as Ben's brother-in-law could have told him.

"But you promised it would be ready at four. I'm due out in Murren right now!"

Abby Carr's cheeks glowed with the intensity of her feelings. Her eyes sparkled. But to Joe, the mechanic, and Duane, the service manager, she was just another complaint.

"Mrs. Carr," Duane tried again. "I explained we'd have it ready if we had the parts. But it turned out—"

"You promised!" she wailed. "My husband's still in Washington and I don't know what to do. I simply have to get these leaflets out to Murren today. The referendum is day after tomorrow."

Joe did not care about her referendum.

"But it's terribly important," said Abby despairingly. "I have to have a car. Do you think it would help if I talked to Mr. Lundgren?"

"It never hurts."

Lundgren Ford was not in the business of lending automobiles, as prominent signs announced. But Fred made house policy as he went along.

"Sure, Mrs. Carr," he said amiably. "Joe, get the Pinto."

"You want us to put stickers on it, too?" Duane asked wearily.

Abby's Gran Torino had lost its ignition system, but it still had plenty of reading material on windows and bumpers.

ATOMS ARE DANGEROUS TO YOUR HEALTH
KEEP BUCKEYE AWAY FROM CHILDREN
VOTE NO!

"Oh, that's wonderful!" she said with radiant gratitude. "But you see there are all these volunteers who have to be ferried out to Murren. And I've got cartons and cartons. I thought Paul was going to be back today, and we could have used his wagon. But he just called to say he's going to be delayed. I don't see how I can get everything into a Pinto . . ."

"Get Mrs. Carr a wagon," said Fred patiently.

Once the whirlwind had passed, he had a second thought. Raising his voice above the cavernous din of the garage, he called, "Duane, you live out in Murren, don't you?"

Duane admitted it.

"Did Mrs. Carr convince you to vote against Buckeye?"

"She sure tried," Duane grinned. "But Marlene got in first. And I'm married to her!"

*   *

Other people were making last-minute efforts too.

"Mr. Heisse isn't in his office," Sheridan Ireland's secretary reported.

"Get Vorhees," Ireland rasped.

Mr. Vorhees was not available either.

"Then get Roger Gladstone, at Lomax Tool."

Mr. Gladstone was on a business trip to Kentucky, checking the generator of the Bluegrass Power Station.

Ireland scowled, then placed another call. This one went through like clockwork.

"That you, Gordon? . . . Fine, fine . . . Yes, the Washington thing went pretty well. We had a little trouble—but what's past is past. . . . Fine . . . Yes, the outlook is good. The referendum should be in the bag. . . ."

Ireland listened for a minute or two. Then, with great deliberation, he said, "Well, anything short of ninety per cent is going to be a real disappointment, if you know what I mean. . . . Yes, we're keeping our fingers crossed. . . . Fine, I'll be talking to you again . . ."

*   *

Atomic power plants do not get built by keeping your fingers crossed. So, another telephone conversation took place later that same day.

"Yup, Lorraine got back this afternoon," said George Barry. "Seems to have had a real good time. I'd like to have gotten away myself. But, of course, I couldn't leave the business that long—the way she can leave the station."

Even when gray rain was not pelting the plate glass, George Barry's real estate office did not have the smell of success. The modest furniture was not shabby; photographs of home and acreage pasted on the walls were not curled and yellow with age. But strangers invariably registered the dour atmosphere, not the clean ash trays and the tidy piles of Barry's Real Estate News Letter.

The same was true of George himself. Murren knew he was a good neighbor. It took someone like Sherry Ireland's Gordon to look beyond the harmless self-importance and spot an iron core of grievance.

"What can I do for you, Mr. Gordon?" Barry asked.

Mr. Gordon wanted to know about the referendum.

George was not one of nature's optimists. "Looks pretty good," he grunted reluctantly. "Lorraine and I have contacted just about every registered voter and—"

The phone interrupted at length. Barry shouldered the receiver and groped for a cigar.

"Yes, Mrs. Carr is still handing stuff out," he said finally. "But there's no use your printing up more flyers. In the first place, people here have already made up their minds, or it looks that way to me. Besides, if I spend any more money, people like Lorraine are going to start wondering where it's all coming from. And that could get us all in trouble."

Mr. Gordon did not like the sound of that and Barry pressed his advantage. "I don't like the way the Carrs are talking. They don't have any hopes from the referendum, but they say they're not going to stop there."

Gordon's assignment was the referendum, as he made clear.

"Lorraine and I have already thought of that," George answered him. "I've got the bylaws right here. The public announcement is posted at the firehouse and in the Town Hall. And we've got people already assigned to watch the polling places . . . What's that?"

A cloud of smoke enveloped him as he said his last word.

"Well, you can tell your people there's not a thing to worry about—if you're talking about the election. We'll take care of that. But you mark my words, the election isn't going to be the end of the trouble here in Murren. Not by a long shot!"

*   *

The great day came to Murren and, like most great days, it was a letdown. There was a big turnout. But a big turnout, in Murren, spread over twelve hours, boiled down to knots of three or four voters at any given moment.

There were, however, a lot of other people milling around. The State Police were back again, this time to prevent the recurrence of violence. The FBI was also on hand, still looking for clues to the identity of Davis Quentin's murderer. The press, hoping for the worst, had come from as far away as Chicago. On the sidelines were PEP, the Sierra Club, the American Civil Liberties Union, federal marshalls and several Atomic Energy Commission observers.

The townspeople were outnumbered two to one. But they dutifully appeared to cast their votes and, by ten o'clock that evening, the ballots had been counted.

"We won!" Lorraine Westerfeld crowed.

Murren did not run to victory rallies, much to the disappointment of various reporters and photographers. Down at the Town Clerk's office, everything was pretty quiet; Verna's Coffee Shop had closed, as usual, at eight-thirty. Westerfeld's Texaco Station, between land-office business at the pumps and jubilation around Lorraine's battered desk, was the liveliest place in town.

"That will show those outsiders that this town realizes how much good Buckeye Atomic is going to do," said a lantern-jawed man, counting out the price of a new windshield wiper. "And there's going to be no damned nonsense about a recount. It was ten to one, in our favor!"

Lorraine smiled beatifically until a honk from outside reminded her of business as usual. "Well that," she said with a glint in her eye as she heaved herself up, "should give Paul Carr something to think about!"

CHAPTER 10

But Paul Carr already had more than enough to think about. And by the time he and the Newburg *News* had finished serving subpoenas, everybody in the county realized that the Murren referendum had been the opening, rather than the closing, round of the great Buckeye battle. Up until now, Lorraine Westerfeld and the selectmen of Murren had been fighting on their own turf. Round Two was taking place in Carr's territory.

Lawsuits come in different shapes and sizes. Some are for automobile accidents, some for breach of contract, some for bounced checks. But every lawyer knows the opening moves by heart. First, the plaintiff and defendant deal directly with each other, on a scale of escalating hostility. Then the plaintiff loses his patience and marches off to Gamadge, Gamadge & Gamadge. A menacing letter is dispatched. The defendant, after a horrified squawk, hires Ballantine, Ballantine & Ballantine to read the letter and answer it. Time and money are spent going over the same old ground. Then, at length, the attorneys agree on what everyone else has known all along: There is an irreconcilable conflict.

This respite ends when Mr. Gamadge files a pleading at the county court which recites the wrong suffered by his client. His presentation is so simple, so eloquent, that any impartial observer would give judgment for the plaintiff at once. But scarcely have the carbons been delivered, than Mr. Ballantine comes rattling back with a document of his own. This one leaves no doubt that the defendant, far from being a malefactor, is himself a victim. During this period both parties are striding around their living rooms with chests thrown out, telling their wives that this will show that son-of-a-seacook.

Then, after calculating the exact minute at which these simple pleasures have crested, both lawyers suggest to their clients an out-of-court settlement. The defendant, without admitting the slightest guilt, offers 20 per cent of the damages demanded—simply to avoid the expense and vexation of a trial. The plaintiff, insisting that his injuries cry to heaven for redress, remembers that he too is a busy man. In the interest of expedition, he shaves 20 per cent from his original claim.

The horse trading has begun. From here on, it is anybody's guess. The defendant is closeted with his tax adviser; the plaintiff plans how to spend his windfall. More often than not, a sum leaving both parties feeling cheated is finally agreed upon.

With Paul Carr and editor Henry Hough, things did not work out this way. Both of them thirsted for their day in court. With justice, principle and truth at stake, no sacrifice was too great.

Those they dragged with them into Newburg's Courthouse saw it differently.

"This is a disgrace!" Sheridan Ireland fumed as he moved down the row to make room for Ben Safford and Jim Vorhees. "Do you realize I've had to come all the way from Cincinnati for this farce?"

"We just flew in from Washington," Ben retorted. "And that bunch over there doesn't look local," he added, waving at two solid rows of business suits and attaché cases.

As far as Ireland was concerned, this just proved his point. "If Hough had listened to me, we wouldn't be going through this ridiculous performance," he grumbled.

Ben was curious. "You mean you asked Henry to settle?"

Ireland reddened. "There have been too many headlines about Buckeye already. I told Hough that Tristate would be sympathetic with any attempt to avoid further publicity."

"I'm willing to make a bet about Henry's answer," said Ben with a grin.

Before Sheridan Ireland could erupt, Roger Gladstone intervened from two seats down. "Oh, come on, Sherry. The way I hear it, Paul Carr wouldn't even talk about settling. When somebody is hellbent on suing, there's no sense trying to reason with them."

A Newburg lawyer who had dropped by to see the fun leaned forward with a contribution for Ben's ear only. "He can say that again. Did you know Carr's handling the case himself? That guy won't listen to good advice from anyone."

Before the criticism could continue, the court clerk was heralding the entrance of the judge. The proceedings began and within half an hour, Paul Carr was front and center.

An expert witness had taken the stand, and Carr was asking him about radioactive hazards. Henry Hough's lawyer promptly jumped to his feet, objecting to the line of questioning.

"Your Honor, I submit that this testimony goes to the heart of my case," said Paul Carr passionately. "We will show that the plaintiffs have been pictured as rabble-rousing demagogues, when in fact they were presenting scientifically valid data in the exercise of their right to lawful assembly."

At the defendant's table, attorney Murray Upton put a hand on his client's shoulder. Stirring restively, Henry Hough glared at Carr.

"Furthermore, we will show that the basic facts with respect to Buckeye Atomic have been systematically distorted by the defendant."

"Keep calm, Henry," Murray Upton murmured.

Judge Schloman cocked his head, thought for a moment, then reached a decision. "Well, Counselor, the defendant's treatment of Buckeye Atomic is not in question. But I will admit the evidence as it goes to the defendant's treatment of the plaintiff, provided that you can connect it up later."

Paul Carr smiled, Murray Upton scowled, and Ben turned to his friend the Newburg lawyer. "Say what you like, Roy, Carr got what he wanted."

"Well, he got the door open," Roy conceded grudgingly. He still disapproved of lawyers representing themselves.

Through that open door, Paul Carr called witness after witness, ostensibly to establish the scientific facts, actually to paint Buckeye Atomic as a ticking bomb. The defense, fuming impotently, periodically boiled over with objections. Judge Schloman functioned as linesman, timekeeper and official scorer. It was all very engrossing for the players. The gallery, however, began to wilt.

By the time the noon recess was called, tempers around Ben had deteriorated. Jim Vorhees sounded depressed as he took a reading of the opposition. "My God, those are big names Carr has subpoenaed. Altschuler is probably the world authority on cooling systems. As for Brandenburg—"

"How the hell did Carr round them up at this late date?" an outraged Sheridan Ireland demanded.

Vorhees was thinking ahead. "Carr can't be responsible for this. He doesn't swing enough weight," he drawled. "And if there's anyone masterminding things from behind the scenes, we'd better find out."

He had already risen and was waving toward the departing file of scientists. Two of them stopped in their tracks, smiling broadly.

"You people go on without me," Vorhees said, slipping into the aisle. "The AEC is going to be picking up the lunch tab for those two."

Almost anyone else in the world would have been grateful for Jim Vorhees' prompt maneuvering, thought Ben. But not Sheridan Ireland.

"What does he mean, rushing off that way?" he asked resentfully. "Why didn't he invite those experts to join us?"

"Jim probably thinks he can get more out of them, this way." Roger Gladstone soundeded amused. "After all, he represents the government, not a private company."

"That's just the trouble," Ireland said shortly. "How do we know he'll tell us everything he finds out? He may have his own ax to grind."

There was a rasp in Gladstone's voice when he replied. "Look, Sherry, if the AEC is turning against us, they've got a simple way of letting us know—like withdrawing our license."

"I didn't say the AEC," hissed Ireland in a furious undertone. "I said Vorhees."

"What in hell do you mean by that?"

But Ireland was already regretting his frankness. "How do I

know what's going on?" he evaded. "That's the whole problem. When I have a mess, I like to stay on top of it. The information should come directly to me so I can make the decisions. Now, everybody's running off by themselves."

Ben Safford had had more than enough ego display. "Well, strictly speaking, it isn't your problem," he said. "Henry Hough and the *News* are being sued, not Tristate Electric. I guess Henry's already made that point."

"Hough is too stupid to see that this libel case is part of the big picture," Ireland rejoined. He was still smarting from Henry Hough's rejection. "I will certainly demand that Vorhees tell us whatever he finds out."

He was as good as his word. When they reconvened, he fidgeted nervously until the AEC man appeared, then began firing questions.

"Well? How has Carr gotten all those experts? Is he just fronting for somebody?"

Vorhees held up a hand. "Slow down," he urged. "Give me a chance to answer. And you'd better brace yourself. The man who got all these briefcases here is Dean Humphrey Kennison." He paused dramatically.

There was a long silence.

As far as Ben Safford was concerned, it was the silence of total ignorance. Who the hell was Dean Humphrey Kennison?

Sheridan Ireland recoiled. "I don't like it," he almost moaned. "I don't like it."

Roger Gladstone was also poleaxed. "Well, I'll be damned! How in God's name did Carr swing that?"

"There's nothing mysterious about it, but it sure spells bad luck for us." Vorhees shrugged at the odd tricks of fate. "It turns out that Carr has some kind of connection to Kennison's family."

"And he's been keeping quiet about it?" Gladstone asked incredulously. "That should have been the first thing he hit us with."

Vorhees nodded his agreement. "I don't understand it either. But Altschuler and Brandenburg didn't hear from Kennison until last week."

Ben Safford had been around long enough to know that there

were hundreds of earthshaking names he had never heard of. Ordinarily it did not bother him—not until Newburg was involved.

"And just who is this Kennison?" he asked impatiently.

Vorhees took a deep breath. "As far as position goes, he's Dean of Engineering at Midwestern University. But that doesn't tell you the half of it. Actually he's the outstanding authority on water purification from here to Timbuktu. He already had a reputation thirty years ago, but who cared then? The glamor boys were all in electronics and nuclear science in those days. But now! For the last ten years he's been jetting around as a consultant to all the big power companies, to foreign governments, to UN missions. If you've got a water problem, the first man you try for is Dean Kennison. If he's too busy, the expert you end up with is bound to have studied under him. Everyone in the field has."

"They sure have." Roger Gladstone grinned. "Even me. I worked for him a couple of years after college. Humphrey's quite a guy."

Sheridan Ireland snorted. "Maybe, maybe. But we're not here to clean up some water." He waved around the courtroom, at the jury filing into its box, at the witnesses still settling into their seats. "Sooner or later, they're going to have to stop horsing around. Then they'll get to what happened when the Carrs took their peaceful protest to Murren, and ended up killing an AEC inspector!"

*   *

They got there far too soon for Ben Safford's peace of mind. When Paul Carr finally called him, Ben wanted to break and run.

"My next witness is Congressman Benton F. Safford."

The middle initial, thought Ben as he trudged to the stand, was a giveaway. It could only mean that Carr was building him up in order to knock him down. The one consolation was the lack of audience. Lunch and the tedium of the morning session had shaken out the idle curiosity seekers.

Methodically, Paul Carr took Ben over his activities in Murren.

"So, you never left the building, Congressman?"

"I did not."

"You did not see Davis Quentin leave the building?"

"I did not."

"You did not see the protesters between your arrival at seven-thirty and your departure at ten-thirty?"

"I did not."

"Then, wouldn't you say that anything could have happened outside without your knowledge, that Davis Quentin could have met anybody at all, that there are no grounds for alleging that the protesters were responsible for his death?"

Ben would have been happy to reply, but Murray Upton decided to show the flag.

"Your Honor!" he protested. "Counsel is asking a leading question of his own witness. I object."

Paul Carr had been waiting for this moment.

"Your Honor!" He pointed at Ben. "I demand the right to treat Congressman Safford as a hostile witness."

"The witness is not related to the defendant or joined with him in any enterprise . . ."

"The witness is demonstrably biased in favor of the defendant . . ."

Ben felt more and more like the rope in a tug of war. As the lawyers snarled and feinted over his meaningless contribution, all other heads swiveled to examine him. He knew he did not make an impressive spectacle. Janet's expression was enough to tell him so. Well, her turn would come.

"Objection overruled," Judge Schloman finally snapped.

"Congressman Safford," said Carr sternly, "I am waiting."

Ben blinked. "I've forgotten the question."

While Carr formulated a substitute, Ben recalled the standard advice to witnesses—say as little as possible.

"Certainly," he answered when the time came.

For a moment, Paul Carr hesitated. Then, his voice curt, he turned aside.

"I am through with this witness," he said with controlled contempt.

The judge inclined his head to the defendant's table. "Do you wish to cross-examine, Counselor?"

Murray Upton was too shrewd to drag things out. He was satisfied with a description of Ben's arrival at Murren to find pickets milling around, and the subsequent ejection of the Carrs.

Sooner or later a witness was going to give Paul Carr a fight about the responsibility for Davis Quentin's death. Until then, Murray Upton was holding his fire.

Nobody had to wait long. Ben had barely cleared the chair before Paul Carr was showing his teeth in a tight grin.

"I call Sheridan Ireland as my next witness."

CHAPTER 11

Ireland was a hostile witness in all senses of the word. He fought every inch of the way.

"No, I did not see Quentin before the meeting," he said, red-faced with anger. "That mob on the green made it hard to park. We were a couple of minutes late."

Paul Carr's strategy was to goad Ireland. "So, you're claiming that members of PEP were responsible for the disorder in Murren that night?"

"I'm not claiming anything! Everyone knows they were!"

"Well, you were there, Mr. Ireland. Now, will you tell this court what you actually saw and heard them do?"

"I saw them stage a riot, that's what I saw," Ireland shot back. "At the beginning, a bunch of those hooligans were milling around outside the Grange, with picket signs. Then, halfway through the evening, a couple of you who had forced your way inside tried to break up the meeting. It was later, when your people started throwing rocks and smashing windows, that the police said it wasn't safe for us to leave."

"I see." Carr was silky. "Now let's try and figure out what this testimony of yours really amounts to, Mr. Ireland."

"It amounts to what I said!"

"Then, suppose you tell us what you actually saw when you arrived in Murren?"

"I saw a mob."

"Did anybody in this so-called mob threaten you, or assault you?"

"No, but—"

Carr swept forward. "Did anybody prevent your entry into the Grange Hall?"

"No, but—"

"Did anybody even try to speak to you?"

"They didn't have to," Ireland snapped. "Their signs made it plain enough what they had to say."

"And what did they say?"

"A lot of crazy nonsense about atomic explosions and radioactive leaks."

Paul Carr pounced. "In fact, they were warning the community about the very same dangers this court heard a number of eminent scientists testify to this morning."

Ireland could only glare at him.

The examination continued remorselessly. Carr used every weapon at his command to distinguish Ireland's version of what had happened from the actual facts, skillfully modulating from irony to sarcasm to rebuke.

"So, when you say we forced our way inside, it turns out that we walked up the steps, turned the doorknob, and went into the Grange. Tell me, Mr. Ireland, just how did you get into the building."

"That's different."

"So it would seem. When you do it, we're not to call it breaking and entering. Now, you say that my wife and I tried to break up the meeting."

"You demanded the right to speak," Sheridan Ireland said with naked dislike.

"And when the chairman refused, what did we do?"

"You left."

Paul Carr took the jury into his confidence. "That doesn't sound like a riot, does it?"

It seemed to go on for hours. With growing truculence, Ireland was forced to admit that he could not identify the rock throwers, that the protesters had disbanded on official request, that the police had not suggested any threat to his personal safety. Murray Upton's interruptions were not very helpful. Again and again he rose to object. Again and again, Judge Schloman ordered question and answer stricken from the record. But Paul Carr was unruffled. He did not care about the record.

He was painting an indelible picture of a man so swayed by prejudice and self-interest that he was willing to twist any situation into a vilification of the plaintiffs.

Ben wondered whether Carr realized he was simultaneously painting a vivid self-portrait, as well.

"So, it boils down to this, Mr. Ireland," he twisted the knife. "You saw the plaintiffs engaged in peaceful assembly, petitioning for a redress of grievance. And just how real and pressing that grievance is, we have heard from no less an authority than Dr. Joseph Altschuler. That is all you saw, but you do not hesitate to stigmatize their conduct as mob violence. In case you are interested, Mr. Ireland, they were exercising their rights as free-born American citizens. I have no further questions."

As he stepped down, Sheridan Ireland was mopping his brow. But in the row behind the defendant's table, they were not sympathetic.

"The damned fool," George Barry snarled. "He's going to sink us all. Why doesn't someone shut him up?"

Henry Hough slewed around to address his well-wishers. "He's torpedoed our whole case. Whose side is he on?"

"Don't worry, Henry," said Lorraine Westerfeld soothingly. "It doesn't make any difference what the jury thinks of Ireland. You're the defendant."

Henry, and George Barry, interpreted this as meaningless womanly support, but Mrs. Westerfeld had been circulating. "Don't worry," she insisted. "The tide is about to turn. Carr has subpoenaed the state police. Wait until he gets to Tommy Youngman."

State Police Lieutenant Youngman's examination began smoothly enough to lull Paul Carr into overconfidence.

"You regarded the situation in Murren as a simple traffic problem, Lieutenant?"

"Yes, sir."

Lieutenant Youngman duly agreed that small communities were not the best sites for great public events. Yes, local facilities were strained; yes, people had parking difficulties.

"But aside from these inevitable problems, you anticipated no trouble from the presence of the plaintiffs?"

"No, sir."

"And when someone—as yet unknown—instigated disorderly conduct, you had no difficulty clearing the area?"

"No, sir."

On the side lines, Lorraine Westerfeld was holding her breath as Paul Carr marched closer and closer to the unseen pit.

"And when the discovery of Davis Quentin's body was made, you began an investigation, a very thorough investigation?"

"Yes, sir."

"The FBI has assisted you in this investigation?"

"Yes, sir."

"And in spite of the great resources of our own Ohio State Police, and those of the Federal Bureau of Investigation, no arrest has been made?"

"That is correct."

"Then we can say, can we not, that up to this very day nobody knows who was responsible for the disorder in Murren that resulted in confusion, property damage and, tragically, in death?"

"Not exactly."

Paul Carr had already begun swinging toward the jury for his peroration. "What's that?" Caught in mid-turn, he jerked the question over his shoulder.

"We don't know who committed the murder, sir, but we do know who threw one of the rocks."

Clearly Carr did not like the terrain. But he asked the question he had to ask.

"Who was that?"

"A sixteen-year-old boy."

"Ah!" Carr let himself relax too soon. "You mean the police suspect a juvenile who was drawn to the scene by the excitement?"

"No, sir. I mean the boy was seen throwing the rock by one of my officers and by his own parents. He has admitted he was responsible for the drugstore window and his parents have agreed to pay for it. No charge has been filed."

For a moment, Paul Carr hesitated. But the damage had been done. He had gone too far to withdraw.

"And who are the boy's parents?"

"Mr. and Mrs. Robert Greene," said Youngman apologetically. "They are members of the executive board of PEP."

"I see," said Carr quickly, trying to tamp down on the rustle of speculation that ran through the courtroom. "And why was this fact kept secret from the public?"

"Very fortunately, my officer and Mr. Greene both saw the rock go through the drugstore window. As the boy's action could have nothing to do with Davis Quentin's death, my superiors felt it would be unfair to publicize the name of a juvenile in connection with a murder."

"I am sure we all applaud the principle," said Paul Carr evenly. "We'll have to wait and see if it has been in the best interests of justice. Now, Lieutenant, let me revise my earlier question. To this day, you have no idea who murdered Davis Quentin?"

Lieutenant Youngman was as unmoved as ever. "No, sir," he agreed.

It was the best Paul Carr could do before he had to hand Youngman over to Murray Upton. The defense was ready to exploit the opportunity for all it was worth.

First, Upton found three ways to underline the fact that young Greene's delinquency established a link between PEP and the rowdyism in Murren. In passing, he unearthed the information that there had been no window-breaking in Murren for five years.

"Tragic indeed," Upton crooned lovingly, "that such an outbreak of violence should mar so serene a community."

Lieutenant Youngman's men were regularly called to break up drunken brawls in Murren's only beer hall and to investigate marijuana smoking in the school.

"Yes, sir," he said stolidly.

From there, Upton went on to a workmanlike inquiry into the number of PEP supporters who had brought their children.

"You say there were quite a number, Lieutenant? Did anybody explain why?"

Briefly Lieutenant Youngman's control slipped. "One of the mothers explained to me, sir, that children can't be introduced to civic action too early."

For a long moment Murray Upton and the jury were joined in silent communion.

"I don't really understand that, Lieutenant, but I guess you don't either. Now, tell me, what ages were these children?"

Paul Carr, scowling heavily, rose to object. He, Murray Upton and Judge Schloman haggled their way to a more acceptable form of the question. Most of the children had been between twelve and seventeen. And the jury did not like the sound of them—or their parents.

"You say Mr. and Mrs. Greene witnessed their son's conduct? Did they remonstrate with him?"

"Your Honor, what possible bearing can this have . . . ?"

"Your Honor, the plaintiff opened this matter on direct. I have the right to explore on cross . . ."

"Objection overruled."

"No, Mr. Greene did not remonstrate with his son. He remonstrated with my officer."

"In what terms?"

"He wanted to know what right my officer had to speak to his son that way."

"And did Mr. Greene accept responsibility for his son's action?"

"He denied his son's action at that time."

"But subsequently he changed his mind. When was that?"

A thin smile creased Youngman's face. "After Davis Quentin's body was discovered. Then he came down to the station and said he saw the rock go through the window."

In contrast to the policeman, Murray Upton was smiling from ear to ear.

"Thank you very much, Lieutenant. I have no further questions."

Adjournment for the day came not a minute too soon for the plaintiffs.

Roy, the Newburg lawyer sitting behind Ben, was jubilant at having his prophecies fulfilled.

"And what makes it ten times worse, is having it come out of the mouth of Carr's own witness," he chortled.

"Yes, yes I see that—" Ben began unsuccessfully.

"Upton didn't even have to wait for cross. Carr did the damage on his own direct examination," Roy said in a glaze of satisfaction.

But Ben Safford had practiced law once himself. "That's fine, as far as it goes. But you can't tell me that Murray Upton is just waiting for Carr to make mistakes. He must have some ammunition of his own."

"Sure, and it doesn't take second sight to tell what he's aiming at." Roy waggled an instructive finger. "He got that PEP letterhead admitted—the one listing the Greenes on the executive board. That's his target, take my word for it."

What Roy figured out that afternoon, Paul Carr belatedly realized twenty-four hours later. The reason for his slowness had nothing to do with his legal skill. He was the victim of a psychological block.

As far as Carr was concerned, he was the chief executive and spokesman for PEP, which otherwise consisted of a band of nameless members. If the Newburg *News* claimed that PEP had misbehaved, then they had to prove that he, Paul S. Carr, had misbehaved. He had long since forgotten that PEP, as its letterhead proclaimed, had a large executive board and officers galore.

Murray Upton spent the next day capitalizing on this fact. The Greenes, it turned out, were not the only members of PEP's executive board with a rock-throwing son. But Upton's finest hour came with the production of Jonathan Fewling on the witness stand. Fewling, a rangy shambling young man, admitted that he had led the charge to hoist a mushroom cloud from the town flagpole. Beaten back by the Murren defenders and finally warned off by the police, he had fired a few rocks through windows to relieve his feelings. Slumped low in the chair, with his bony knees spread wide, his dirty sneakers tucked out of sight and his thumbs hooked into his garrison belt, he was completely unrepentant.

"Man, I didn't go all the way to Hicksville to palaver with the fat cats," he confided to the jury.

Jonathan, otherwise PEP's Co-ordinator of Student Activities, was worth his weight in gold to Murray Upton, who kept him on the stand as long as humanly possible. It was during the endless questions and answers that Paul Carr learned for the first time that Jonathan had ceased to be a student before the letterheads ever came back from the printer.

"I didn't dig the scene there. Too bourgeois, if you know what I mean," he explained grandly.

Every trial is a drama of sorts. That means every judge is a director of sorts. This one had enough sense of theater to realize that Jonathan Fewling's departure from the witness chair made a perfect curtain. Seizing his gavel, he intoned, "This court is adjourned until ten o'clock Monday morning."

All in all, the day had been a real object lesson to the Carrs.

CHAPTER 12

For Abby, of course, it was a lesson in betrayal. She was still young enough to believe that people pledged to a good cause necessarily embodied all virtue. When cracks appeared in the façade of the Greenes and Jonathan Fewling, only one conclusion was possible. Their commitment to a pure environment had been nothing but pretense.

Her husband was more realistic. To do him justice, Paul Carr recognized that he had mismanaged his case. And while he had every intention of continuing to handle the affairs of PEP, he was not above trying to pick someone else's brains. Accordingly, he seized the first opportunity to join his usual luncheon circle, a group of young lawyers. They were suitably somber when he appeared.

"It doesn't look good, Paul," said one of them. "I had to go downtown yesterday, and I dropped in at the courthouse."

Paul gave a forced smile. "I don't have a chance in hell."

There was a general sigh of relief. His friends had been afraid he expected a show of optimism. The rolypoly one took up his cue.

"It was your own people who scuttled you. It's a shame you didn't examine them before trial."

"It wouldn't have done any good," Carr said brusquely, thinking of Bob and Liz Greene. "They would have lied to me."

"They sure would have," chimed in a new voice. Nick Jesilko looked into his one year of experience. "Witnesses always do."

He was the only trial lawyer in the group, and the others were very respectful.

People are almost always trying to make themselves look too good," he continued, lighting a pipe and leaning back. "Why, I remember one case . . ."

Paul Carr suppressed his impatience during the anecdote. Jesilko was his real hope for constructive suggestions, but Nick had sat through too many discussions of estate plans and tax schemes not to extract his pound of flesh. His story lasted a long time.

Rolypoly brought them back to the issue. "Yeah, Nick, but what does Paul do now? His whole game plan has been wrecked."

"There's still time," Jesilko said enigmatically. "The case hasn't gone to the jury yet."

"What difference does another day make?" demanded Carr. "The jury can't wait to clobber me, ever since they saw that kid Fewling."

"Oh, they're going to clobber you all right. Forget about the jury. What you've got to do is lure the court into error," said Jesilko enthusiastically. "Then you'll have grounds for an appeal. And, remember, whatever else happens, your big chance is the judge's instructions to the jury."

His audience was warming to his theme.

"Then Paul had better draft his own set of instructions, right?" said Rolypoly.

"Absolutely. And, Paul, make them strong enough so he doesn't use them. Then object to every departure from your language—and get those objections into the record!"

Rolypoly was awed. "Fantastic!" he breathed.

"Wonderful!" echoed the others.

Only Paul Carr was silent.

*   *

When he reported to Abby, Paul was derisive.

"Lure the court into error, make a record for appeal," he mimicked. "Who the hell does he think he's talking to?"

The Watergate trials had not been wasted on Abby.

"But, Paul, people do it all the time," she protested. "They must think it's a good idea."

Paul slowed down. "Look, honey, it's different if you're a defendant who's lost in court. Then an appeal can really do something for you. If the verdict is tossed out, then you don't have to go to jail or pay damages or whatever it was. With luck, you're home free. But when you're the plaintiff, things are different. The most you can hope for is the chance to have a new trial. When Jesilko talks about appeals, he's lost his marbles."

"I thought you always said Nick was a good trial lawyer."

"Nick works for an insurance company," Paul said more loudly than he intended. He had decided not to tell Abby one reason against an appeal. Woodruff & Jones was already edgy enough. If he started camping out in Columbus, they were going to wonder why they paid him a salary. Fortunately there was other ammunition. "He doesn't have to think about money. Appeals are expensive, and we can't afford one. You'd be surprised at the cost of a trial transcript."

Here, however, Abby was sure of herself. "We wouldn't pay for it!" she cried, outraged. "PEP would. We can have a fund-raising meeting right away."

Paul opened his mouth to disagree, then closed it. After Murren and the debacle in court, he had vowed never to appear publicly again with members of PEP. In the future he was going to concentrate on solo negotiations behind closed doors. But when he found himself across a conference table from Buckeye and the AEC, he wanted as many weapons as possible. Let the world think he was planning an appeal to the highest court in the state of Ohio. Let the world know that legions of his supporters were writing checks.

"That's not a bad idea," he decided. "At least we can give it a try."

Abby's face lit up. "It will work, you'll see. When should we have the meeting?"

Paul smiled down at her eagerness. "Hey!" he cried in mock alarm. "You can't appeal until you've lost. What about Thursday? The verdict will be in by then, and you'll have time to let everybody know."

"Fine. I'll start telephoning tomorrow." Abby was lost in calculations when another thought occurred. "In fact, it couldn't be better. I forgot to show you the cable that came. Daddy will be here!"

The smile froze on Paul's face. There was only one cloud marring his domestic horizon, and that was his distinguished father-in-law. To be honest, it was not so much Dean Humphrey Kennison as it was Abby's attitude toward her father. She did not realize that he was just another middle-aged, middle-class member of the generation that had made the world so rotten. She could join Paul in freely condemning the senior Carrs. She could see all the flaws in the aunt and uncle who had raised her. But her father was topped by a big shiny halo.

Humphrey Kennison had reacted to his wife's untimely death by looking for a foreign assignment in which to drown his sorrow. As Jim Vorhees had observed, he could not have timed his return to field work better. To Abby he became a remote figure, occasionally descending from some romantic locale in a shower of exotic presents. No wonder she did not associate him with the humdrum failings of affluent suburbia.

And Paul was fair-minded enough to concede that, unless you indicted the man simply because he was a parent, it was hard to come up with a specific accusation. Kennison's status as a widower spared him the flaws of middle-aged marriage. It was impossible to call him a racist when he spent his entire working life with a horde of technicians who were black, brown and yellow. Even red, thought Paul bitterly, remembering when Abby had shocked her aunt and uncle by spending the summer with him on a Navajo reservation. Her father had sent them warm encouragement (from Bechuanaland) and introductions to two tribal chieftains. And warmongering was out, too. Dean Kennison had supported a united Vietnam years before most Americans had heard the word—for reasons centering entirely on the proper utilization of the Mekong River. It was, Paul decided, like having Albert Schweitzer for a father-in-law. You might admire the man, but you didn't like competing against him for your wife's admiration.

But three years of marriage had left their mark.

"That's great," Paul said. "Just great."

*   *

Thursday night was even worse than Paul Carr expected. The shades of Bob and Liz Greene and Jonathan Fewling would not rest. They haunted every other sentence. When Abby discussed duplicating the form letter she had prepared, somebody remembered that Xeroxing had always been done at Bob's office by Bob's secretary. Then it turned out that mailing costs had traditionally been raised from campus students by young Fewling.

"God knows what he told them," remarked a wife who had seen Jonathan on the witness stand.

"With luck, we'll never know," growled her husband.

To cap these horrors, a dark intense man who had not opened his lips in eighteen months suddenly became voluble about the irregularity in PEP's present organization. It was necessary, he insisted, that the renegades send in formal resignations so that new elections could be held.

Paul Carr could not help shuddering. All they needed was more officers to get them into more hot water.

"We can go into that some other time," he said repressively.

But tonight nothing could silence Sidney.

"Now, I'm no lawyer," he said with a modesty that fooled nobody, "but we could get into real trouble. What if Bob Greene wrote a big check on the PEP account?"

"There's eleven dollars in that account," objected someone.

"That makes it even worse," cried Sidney.

It took an hour for him to exhaust the perils he could foresee.

And finally, just as Paul Carr was outlining his plans for an appeal, the meeting was disrupted by Dean Kennison's arrival. His flight had been two hours late. By the time he had apologized, chairs had been shuffled and a host of introductions effected, Paul had lost what little momentum he had.

Still, he was willing to keep trying.

"I was just explaining to the others, Humphrey, how much we'll need in the war chest for an appeal."

"So you lost at the trial? That's too bad, but Abby sounded as if she was expecting it."

"There were a number of difficulties in court," said Paul steadily, hoping that Sidney would not insist on listing them. "But we have good grounds for thinking an appeal will succeed."

"I'm sorry I didn't know what you kids were up to sooner." Kennison half-turned to face his daughter. "You know, honey, I was upcountry when you wrote. I didn't get your letter until I got back to Kuala Lampur, and then I had to catch the first plane to Rome. But I called Joe Altschuler and Charlie Brandenburg as soon as I landed. Did they get here all right?"

"Do you mean Dr. Altschuler is a friend of yours?" asked someone in a thrilled voice.

Dean Kennison was indulgent. "The whole bunch of them are ex-students of mine. I hope they did the old man proud."

Paul Carr knew his duty. "They made very effective witnesses."

Kennison grinned. "I'll bet. Joe can sound like God Almighty when he puts his mind to it." He gave himself a small shake. "Well, that's all right for fun and games, but now we have to get down to business. We don't want to let this libel suit deflect us."

"I don't know exactly what you mean, Humphrey." Paul was testing the water cautiously. "Of course, we're willing to pursue other avenues, such as negotiation."

"All in good time." Kennison had produced a small notebook. "Now the first thing to do is find out whether or not this proposed atomic installation actually does pose any threat."

"Daddy!" Abby's eyes were round with indignation. "It's going to pollute the whole county!"

"Well, of course it is. Everything is a pollutant. You're a pollutant."

"Me!"

"Yes, just sitting there and breathing, you're pouring all the waste products of your respiratory system into the atmosphere. But so long as you stay out of the Black Hole of Calcutta, you're not posing any threat. The atmosphere can take it. Now, when you heat your house or drive your car, you're more of a menace. But that's to be expected. Only very primitive societies with very sparse populations pollute at a low enough level so that nature can handle it unassisted."

It was a mistake to mention primitive societies.

"But that's just the point." It was the passionate voice of one of the founding members of PEP. "The aim of our organization is to recreate the natural unpolluted environment in which man flourishes."

Like all teachers, Dean Kennison had learned the value of using one student in his class as straight man. "It's a great error to think that man automatically flourishes in an unpolluted environment. There are millions of Touaregs dying in the unpolluted Sahara right now. And you can say the same for India and other areas. Very often it boils down to a choice between pollution and starvation."

He had his audience in the palm of his hand. They were comfortable with broad sweeping generalizations, they were impressed by the underlying technical expertise, and they were excited by the novelty of his views. All of them, except Paul Carr.

"You're talking theory, Humphrey. But you don't know these people we're fighting, the way we do. I tell you they'd poison all of Ohio just to make a filthy dollar."

"Sure they would," said Kennison cordially. "Quite a lot of people would. And not just for a filthy dollar. You should see what the Russian developers did to Lake Aral before they were stopped. Fortunately, that situation is being reversed. So you see, it's all a matter of degree. And the first thing for me to do is run around some of the existing installations in the Midwest and see what the pollutant level is."

Carr's jaw had set grimly. "And what good will it do to study some old nuclear plants?"

"To set up our tables of comparative data. We'll see which ones are working at a tolerable pollution level. And while I'm here, I'd better run up to Murren and take a look at the river they're planning to use in the coolant system." He chuckled at his own ignorance. "Would you believe it? I don't even know its name."

"And once you've convinced yourself that there's a genuine peril?" Carr asked in a steely tone.

Kennison looked up, surprised. "Well, if what they're proposing is really out of line, then we'll have to stop them. But you can forget all this business about libel suits and dealing with the local utility—Buckeye or Sunflower or whatever it's called. We'll go straight to the top."

There was a hum of approval.

"And that is where I can help you," said Kennison, generously overlooking the fact that all the preliminary work would be his. "Because it will be a matter of contacts. The scientific community is no problem. And I don't think I'll have much trouble getting to your senators." He was again busy with his notebook. "And we mustn't forget your congressman. It's amazing what a House committee can do if it wants to."

Paul Carr would have had to be a fool not to recognize that the focal point of the room had shifted from his own position, backed up against the mantel, to Humphrey Kennison's easy chair, approximately ten minutes after the dean's arrival.

And it did not take any imagination to foretell how senators and scientists would react. Somehow the great Murren controversy had to be shifted into another arena and stripped of tables of comparative data.

The first stirrings of an idea encouraged Paul to lean back and relax. After all, as his distinguished father-in-law said, it was all a matter of contacts.

CHAPTER 13

By the next day, Humphrey Kennison was going full steam ahead. When the phone on Paul's desk rang, it was now New York, or Columbus or Chicago returning a call. Instead of shopping lists and recipes, the bulletin board in Abby's kitchen bristled with messages: "Daddy—call Dr. Mailer, 617-354-0626," "Tristate Research Facility—4:00 Tuesday."

Paul was morosely studying these thumbtacked scraps when Abby backed through the screen door, almost lost behind two grocery bags.

"Oof!" she said, depositing her burden next to the sink. "I just ran into Romano's for a small roast—and look!"

When she turned to Paul, he had banished the sag from his shoulders and was smiling back at her.

"Here, I'll help." He put a head of lettuce into the refrigerator before adding, "Where's Humphrey?"

"I think he said he was going out to Murren this afternoon," she said, studying a package of cake mix with a puzzled frown. "He said something about taking a look at the Buckeye site."

"Oh, I see," said Paul neutrally.

Abby was happy and excited, and she assumed Paul was too. Her afterthought came innocently. "What did you do this afternoon, Paul? Did you call Nick Jesilko?"

"No," he said more shortly than he intended. "That's just a waste of time."

"Still—"

"No, I got thinking about what Humphrey was saying last night about contacts. You know, I've got a few of my own." Her wide-eyed expectancy made him feel better. "Humphrey knows all the wheels at the AEC. But right now, my pipeline may be more useful. Anyway, it's worth a try. I'm going to grab the morning plane to Washington—just to see what I can do."

"I didn't know you had a pipeline to the AEC," she marvelled. "Oh Paul, tell me all about it."

With a few important omissions, he did so.

*   *

Humphrey Kennison approved of Paul's plan. Abby was thrilled by it. Buoyed by their support, Paul felt reinvigorated until he touched down at National Airport the following morning. But then and there, the twinges began.

Nina Yeager only made them worse.

"Why on earth did you keep Kennison up your sleeve so long?" she asked, handing him a huge, earthenware mug of coffee.

"Do you have any cream?" he muttered.

"Afraid not," she said cheerfully. "Don't try to duck, Paul. Jim Vorhees came back from Ohio frothing at the mouth. Is it true that Kennison's a relative of yours?"

"He's my father-in-law," Paul retorted sulkily, taking refuge in Nina's bitter black brew.

"God, you had all the trumps, and you threw them away."

"What kind of trump is he, when he's always in Zaire?" Paul defended himself.

She was impatient with his slowness. "You didn't have to produce him, you know. All you had to do was let people know he's your father-in-law. Then nobody would have dared treat you like a crackpot. Buckeye would have been damned respectful—Andy Heisse and Jim would have seen to that. With Humphrey Kennison on your side, ERDA might have thought twice before they issued that damned permit."

Anxious to drop the subject, he said, "Well, that's water over the dam."

But she did not let him off so lightly. "You should have done something before Andy Heisse took a stand. Now he's got to back it up. That's the way things are here in Washington, if you want to avoid trouble on the Hill."

None of this conversation was going the way Paul had expected. Back when they were law students together, Nina had been a diffident pretty girl, eager to please. Now everything about her was dramatic—the oversize glasses, the cool contradictions, the sweeping gestures. For the first time Paul noticed her determined jaw line. Thank God, he thought unguardedly, for Abby's fine-boned delicacy.

But that spurt of gratitude made him squirm inwardly. Paul had not actually lied to Abby. But his version of the literal truth had not included Nina Yeager, or the boldly contemporary apartment in Alexandria. Not that there was really anything to know. But, somehow or other Paul knew that Abby would not like Nina. Smarting from her strictures Paul was not sure he did either.

"Talking about trouble on the Hill," he snapped, in an effort to reassert himself, "we may be causing some ourselves."

But his resumé of Humphrey Kennison's projected political overtures misfired.

"Interesting," she said ambiguously, shoving her glasses to the top of her head. "Of course, I don't know how much clout he's got up there. Most scientists do better with the agencies, where they can always talk to an expert. Still, Kennison knows his way around." Down came the glasses again. "But Paul, that leaves you out in the cold, doesn't it?"

Paul gritted his teeth. "Sure it does. That's why I want to know if you can think of any way of getting to Heisse—"

"The place for you," she interrupted, "is Columbus, Ohio."

"Columbus?" he repeated. "Why? State government doesn't have anything to say about Buckeye, Nina."

"That's just it," she overrode him. "Look, Kennison's going to take over the whole technical fight, isn't he? From where I sit, that looks like a standoff. Maybe he'll make a dent—but then again, maybe he won't. Say what you will about the agency, we've got some pretty high-powered people, too. Either way, there's nothing in it for you. But there is another angle that's right up your alley. If Buckeye is dangerous, it's a threat to a broader area than Murren, or even Newburg County. Why not claim that it's criminal to leave the decision to local government?

Plenty of states are taking that power away from the villages and towns. You should start a movement to have Ohio do it, too!"

This was even worse than Nick Jesiklo's legal advice, and Carr said so. "Sure! And with luck, I get legislation years after Buckeye has gone into operation. The reason I'm here is to stop Buckeye now, and the place to do that is the AEC."

She narrowed her eyes. "For an ambitious guy, you're playing a damned funny game."

"All right, I'm ambitious," he said quickly. "But, Nina, I'm serious about this fight, and I'm not overlooking any chance I get."

"You're never going to get Heisse to reverse himself," she said baldly. "There's only one thing that could do that—the murder."

He stared at her. "What's that supposed to mean?"

"Have you forgotten Davis Quentin?" she asked softly.

Paul had not forgotten Davis Quentin. He had pushed him to the back of his mind. For days he had lived with the dread of what the police might discover. But nothing had happened. By now he had convinced himself that nothing would.

"The police have given up on Davis Quentin," he said warily. "They probably realize that they made a mistake, that it was an accident, after all."

"Don't you believe it! The FBI is busy as hell. Once they found out that Dave got onto something in Murren, something that made him want to hightail it back to headquarters, they were on our necks. And they still are."

This was the first time Carr had heard about Davis Quentin's sudden decision to fly to Washington.

"Well, maybe that explains everything," he said slowly. "Maybe Quentin was bribed to okay Buckeye, and wanted more than the traffic would bear. Or maybe he found out that Buckeye wasn't safe, and had to be silenced! Either way, the murderer—"

"Oh, grow up!" she said with contempt. "Dave Quentin was a safety inspector for operating plants. He didn't have anything to do with okaying Murren—and there was nothing there for him to see."

Before he could marshal his arguments, she swept on, "Look, Paul, Dave Quentin was just in Murren to give a PR talk. But he was a pretty savvy guy. Maybe he stumbled onto something."

"Like what?" he asked defiantly.

"Like finding out that Sheridan Ireland bribed someone in Washington. Or that Tristate was blackmailing some selectman. How should I know? But if Dave uncovered something really dirty, then you could, too. That way the AEC would be forced to take another long look at the situation. Understand?"

He was not altogether sure that he did. "You mean, I should take up where he left off?"

She nodded.

"Not on your life," he said firmly. "I'm keeping as far from murder as I can. The last thing I want to do is tangle with the FBI any more than I have to."

For a moment she sat still, hands locked across her knees. Then, with a half-smile, she said, "You'd better brace yourself."

He looked up suspiciously.

"I told you the FBI was all over us, didn't I?" she said dispassionately. "You want to bet they already know who's been tipping you off about Heisse and Tristate?"

"But Nina," he protested, "we've been careful about being seen together. How could anybody link us up?"

Once again, she was older and wiser than he was. "We've been careful, if you're talking about a citizen's protest against a nuclear power plant," she shrugged. "When it comes to a murder investigation, we might just as well have hired a hall and invited the public."

While he struggled with this threat, she added, "I'm going to take care of myself, Paul. I'd advise you to do the same."

*   *

"Oh, I'm glad you got back so soon," Abby greeted him that evening. "Do you want anything to eat? There's plenty left over."

"No, they fed us on the plane." Paul paused, with his tie in one hand, his jacket in the other. Putting two and two together he said, "Where's Humphrey? Didn't he eat with you?"

"He called a couple of hours ago. He went out to Murren again, and he decided to have dinner with someone there."

Paul was relieved that he did not have to face a critical audience. Instead of going upstairs, he sank into the nearest chair and stretched. "This was one helluva day."

Abby was neatly curled up on the sofa. "Didn't it go well?" she asked solicitously.

"Oh, I picked up some information, all right," he said cautiously. "But I don't think the AEC is going to help us out—not one little bit."

After a covert look at his drawn face, Abby did not press him for further details.

But this respite proved short-lived. By the next morning, Paul was under fire.

Dean Kennison was late for breakfast. But it was Sunday, so this put him only a step behind Paul and Abby. One glass of orange juice was enough to get him going.

"And why did you neglect to tell me the most important item in this whole Buckeye situation?" he asked severely.

"What in the world are you talking about, Daddy?" replied Abby from the stove where she was scrambling eggs.

"You forgot to mention that Davis Quentin was murdered."

Paul had been braced for something like this. "No we didn't, Humphrey," he said from behind the Sunday paper. "That's how the Newburg *News* libeled us. They said we were responsible for Quentin's death."

Humphrey Kennison was not going to split hairs. "I was given the distinct impression that there was a rock-throwing fracas in which Quentin was accidentally killed. Nobody said anything about premeditated murder."

Abby shared none of Paul's qualms. "Oh, Daddy, that was just a theory the police had!"

"Nonsense!" Kennison thundered. "Haven't you bothered to listen to the police releases? Quentin was deliberately murdered."

Abby turned off the fire and, after a moment, Paul lowered his paper. But it was she who took up the cudgels. "What difference does that make? It doesn't change anything about Buckeye, Daddy. Of course we're sorry about Inspector Quentin. But we'd be sorry for him if it was an accident, too."

This reasoning irritated her father. "Abby, I am not talking about sympathy. I am talking about facing facts. Murder makes all the difference in the world."

Abby was beginning to sound frightened. She cast an uncertain look at Paul, then said, "But, Daddy, you don't think we killed him, do you?"

"Tchaa!" In disgust, Kennison slammed down his glass. "How can you be so obtuse? There is something very fishy about Buckeye, something far worse than degrees of pollution."

With an effort, Paul forced himself to speak. "Naturally I understand the implications of Quentin's murder, Humphrey," he said, hearing himself as if from a distance. "But if you're suggesting that it could be used as a lever in dealing with the AEC, I don't see how."

"What's wrong with you two?" Kennison erupted. "What is so hard to understand? A woman without a college education had no difficulty in following me. Mrs. Westerfeld agrees that—"

"Mrs. Westerfeld!" Abby choked.

Her father continued implacably. "She and I agreed at once. Where there is a cesspool, you don't talk about maneuvering—or levers, as you put it, Paul. There's only one thing to be done— clean it up!"

Abby had not even heard him. "Daddy, what were you doing with Mrs. Westerfeld?" she cried accusingly.

He blinked at her. "What would I be doing with her? We had dinner together."

"How could you?" Abby wailed.

Paul was scowling at his coffee, summarizing the experience of twenty-four hours.

"God damn all women!"

CHAPTER 14

For all his newfound misogyny, Paul Carr had not yet tangled with a real tigress. Women need time to hit their stride. Someone like Elsie Hollenbach could have eaten him for breakfast.

Mrs. Hollenbach, when she succeeded her late husband, came to Congress with her youth safely behind her. While other freshman legislators struggled to establish distinctive identities, she effortlessly stamped everything she touched. Right from the start there was a Hollenbach way to question witnesses, a Hollenbach response to horsetrading bids, a Hollenbach style for badgering agencies. In short order, everybody knew that Elsie drank martinis and served sherry, lunched on cottage cheese, and kept a stock of fresh corsages in her office refrigerator.

But her outstanding triumph was her spring barbecue. Mrs. Hollenbach was totally uninterested in housekeeping. Her nondescript home in Maryland had been decorated by a department store and she rarely turned on her oven. So, in the normal course of events, Elsie did not entertain. But each spring, in repayment of hospitality, she hired a caterer, ordered mountains of steak, corn and salad, and opened her grounds. And there was the sleeper—for Elsie was a passionate and indefatigable gardener. She had not bought a house but one and a half acres of topsoil. Every square inch was now a piece of perfection. What began as a simple party had turned into a red-letter day for every serious gardener in Washington, and elsewhere.

Even for Mrs. Anthony Martinelli. Dolores Martinelli kept the home fires burning in Providence, Rhode Island, for three hundred and sixty-four days of the year. But, every May, she forgot her low opinion of Washington, took an embittered look at her own rhododendrons, and enplaned south. There were others, even more unexpected, such as Jim Vorhees. Not many people knew that his devotion to the AEC was equalled only by his feeling for rock gardens. The trunk of his car had a special collection box and he drove the George Washington Expressway with an eye cocked for the perfect boulder.

Even the State Department valued Elsie's annual fete. If they had an awkward guest on their hands, they would give Congresswoman Hollenbach a hopeful ring. This was a legacy from the Russian Admiral. He had arrived in Washington for an interminable series of disarmament talks. While young men from the Foreign Service ruthlessly entertained him, he grew more and more melancholy. Finally, somebody decided on desperate measures. One look around the barbecue told the Admiral he was home. With a Slavic roar of delight he had seized an interpreter and buttonholed Elsie for hours. Long after the caterers had cleaned up, he left, clutching a hibiscus seedling in his enormous fist, regarding it with paternal pride.

If the federal government found Elsie's hospitality useful, so did the state of California. This was because of the time, the place and one particular man. The time, of course, was the beginning of summer electioneering. The place—Washington—had the full Golden State congressional delegation on hand. The man had been Speaker of the California House, not only a Democrat but also an aficionado of water gardens. Over the years, so many California officer holders and aspirants had found it worthwhile to turn up, that Elsie's bash had become an unofficial bipartisan summit, where more than one California budget had been finalized. The Speaker had been dead these five years, but politicians are conservative men. They were still caucusing down by the lily pool.

With so many important people attending, everybody else wanted to come too. The Washington *Post* began covering the event. For a single day every year, Elsie Hollenbach was one of Washington's redoubtable hostesses.

Under such circumstances, Ben Safford always looked forward to Elsie's invitation.

"In fact," he said to Val, as they both climbed out of the taxi, "it's the only Washington party where you can never tell who you'll meet."

"You're right. Last time I was here I fetched and carried for a WAC from Camp Pendleton and the First Lady." Val paused appreciatively as a vagrant breeze caressed him. "I don't know what it is, but Elsie's place is always twenty degrees cooler than anyplace else in town."

Ben grinned. "You can say that to me, Val, but don't say it to her. It's got something to do with the way she plants things. If you don't watch out, Elsie will tell you all about it."

"The only thing I intend to ask anybody is the way to the bar." Val had resumed his measured progress and his instinct was as sure as ever. Two magnolias further on and they came to Capitol Caterers, doing a brisk trade.

"Good evening, Oakes," trumpeted a voice from within the mob. "I didn't know you were a regular at these outings."

Val was inclined to be fretful until he had glass in hand. "The trouble with you boys from California, Heisse, is that you never bother to see who else is here."

Recalling Andy Heisse's background, Ben guessed that he was drinking Elsie's gin in a dual capacity. Right now, he was an AEC commissioner. But someday, he might be back in Sacramento.

Val had reached the same conclusion. "Surprised you're not down by the frog pond."

"I guess our meetings have become legendary," Heisse chuckled. "But we always have time to socialize first. And there are other things to think about—ah, here's the waiter."

By the time Ben and Val had been served, Heisse not only had another drink, he had a blonde.

"Nina, I'd like you to meet Congressman Safford from Ohio, and Congressman Oakes, from South Dakota. Nina Yeager is one of our attorneys at the Commission. She did some of the spadework on the Buckeye permit."

Heisse was beaming with generosity as he shared the credit. Of course, Ben thought, a critic might say that he was spreading the blame. Whatever Nina Yeager thought, however, Ben could not tell. Her expression was pleasant, polished and about as informative as one of Elsie's peonies.

"Of course, Nina will have to move on to something else now that the Buckeye formalities are over. I'm sure you've heard how that libel suit in Newburg went."

"I was there," said Ben tersely before changing the topic. "Elsie really does pull them in from all over, doesn't she? I hear that bunch over there is from the Common Market."

But he had reckoned without Miss Yeager. Smoothly, she said, "I'm not so sure the formalities are over, Commissioner Heisse."

This arrested Heisse, who had been prepared to move on. "What's that?" he demanded.

Nina Yeager was not alarmed by his sudden peremptoriness. In fact, she did not even answer him. With a self-possessed smile, she addressed Ben. "You know, I'm from Ohio originally myself."

"Oh, really?" said Ben, marking time. All too often these words were only the prelude.

But she was telling, not asking. "I just happened to run into a friend of mine yesterday—a friend from home. He comes from near Murren. It seems that he's met Dean Kennison."

Val Oakes, rocking on his heels, was hanging on every word as keenly as if fascinated. Pretty girls, Ben knew, frequently had this effect on him. But Andy Heisse was less impressionable.

"Kennison," he blustered gruffly. "Let me tell you, Nina, that Kennison isn't going to make any difference at all. Jim's over-reacting—and I've already told him so. I'll back our people against Kennison any day. We've got nothing to fear from him."

Nobody in his immediate circle burst into applause. Even the arrival of Elsie did not help. Elsie, of course, was capable of eloquent approval of any administrator who maintained morale by reposing confidence in his staff and going to bat for them—particularly when that administrator was a Republican from California. But not today.

"No," she was saying. "I have always considered petunias very unrewarding. I don't have any around."

Dolores Martinelli, to judge from her expression, admired petunias.

"But your floribunda sounds magnificent," Elsie continued with regal graciousness. "I do look forward to seeing it some time. Don't you, Ben? Dolores, have you met . . ."

During the flurry of introductions, Ben let the question lapse. Floribunda at Tony's establishment in Providence paled into insignificance compared to Elsie herself.

Val always had an eye for what the ladies were wearing. "Say, Elsie," he said, "that's a jim-dandy outfit."

She responded with a self-conscious flush. "Well, times change, you know, and one must keep up. I. Magnin simply pleaded with me."

Today Elsie, whose bow to informality had never gone further than white pumps, was wearing a long, flowing saffron-yellow garment that rippled gently in the breeze, from neck to toe. Personally, Ben felt as though he had come on the Statue of Liberty in blue jeans, but he managed to chime in with a compliment of his own.

"Well I will say it's comfortable," she confided, leading him to suspect that Janet would know what she was talking about. Then, raising her voice, she addressed the larger party, "Now, I want you all to come along and admire my flowering cherries. Then, afterwards I can show you my greenhouse."

Val and Ben, who had already seen the cherry trees, managed to elude the tour group that obediently formed.

"Although I've always wanted to ask Elsie if she bullied the Japanese Ambassador." They were moving toward the large marquee where chairs and tables awaited the guests who could tear themselves away from the crape myrtle. Suddenly Val halted, and in an access of courtliness, apologized, "Why I beg your pardon, Miss Yeager. I didn't just see you there."

There was a modicum of surprise in his voice too, and Ben shared it at finding that Nina Yeager was still with them. To cover it, he said, "Can I get you another drink?"

"No, thank you," she replied with composure.

"I guess you've already seen the cherry trees, too," said Val with a practiced twinkle.

"Why yes," she told him. "Jim—Jim Vorhees, that is—insisted that I go take a look at them the minute we got here. I believe you know him, don't you? He's our Deputy Administrator at the AEC."

Val, softhearted to a fault, could not bear to see a pretty young thing work so hard without help. "Why sure I know

Jim," he said largely. "And Ben does, too. He was down there in Newburg, watching you testify about Buckeye, wasn't he, Ben?"

Ben did not even bother to send Val a reproachful look. Obviously, Miss Yeager had something to say. The sooner she said it, the better.

"Yes," he said. "And I heard about Dean Kennison, too."

"Dean Kennison," she echoed as if she had just remembered. "That's what we were talking about before Mrs. Hollenbach came by."

"That's right," Ben agreed. "Andy Heisse was just saying that the AEC really isn't much worried by him."

From somewhere in the distance there was a burst of hearty masculine laughter. If it was the California miniconvention, he thought, they weren't talking presidential politics.

"What I heard," said Nina, "is that Kennison isn't going to be satisfied with tackling the AEC on technical grounds. He's planning a political offensive—"

"His son-in-law has already tried that," said Ben.

"Oh, nothing like PEP," she said loftily. "Kennison's going to pull real strings. The way I understand it, he's mounting a pressure campaign on the Ohio delegation in Washington. I guess you'd be high on his list, Mr. Safford."

If she meant to dismay him, she succeeded.

"God help you, Ben," said Val cheerily. "Say, isn't that Tony sitting all by himself over there?"

"Oh, there's Jim, too," said Nina Yeager artlessly. "I suppose I really should go admire the rock garden. It's been so nice talking to you . . ."

Ben watched her retreat into the festivities with resignation. Nina Yeager did not strike him as the kind who did favors for nothing. What return did she expect for her warning? Or was she prudently building credit in heaven?

Val was still busy with details. "That little lady's got a bee in her bonnet. You notice the way she stuck to you like glue?"

"I noticed," said Ben grumpily. "You don't think that she just wanted to alert me for my own good?"

Val scouted this optimism with open contempt. "Don't you recognize buttering up when you see it?"

"No," said Ben, wending his way past a table from the British Embassy, twittering about herbaceous borders.

"Well, I can," said Val simply. "Question is, was she buttering you up, or buttering her bosses up? It sounds to me as if she's got old Jim Vorhees snaffled."

Ben was pondering what turn further entanglement in the Buckeye mess could take, but he had to protest. "Jim's not so old. And anyway, what does snaffled mean?"

"If you don't know, I don't want to be the one to destroy your innocence. Hello there, Tony . . ."

Unlike some elected officials, Val Oakes could walk, chew gum, talk and think—all at the same time. It helped when the walk was to the bar, but even a marquee would do. He put his glass down beside Tony's and settled comfortably in one of Capitol Caterer's folding chairs.

It was not the same old Tony.

"You're the last man I'd expect to find at a garden party," said Val with one of his rare failures of tact. "I didn't know you were keen on posies, Tony."

Despite his own preoccupation, Ben felt obliged to intervene. Val must have forgotten that Dolores was out there somewhere, gushing over a fringed verbena. Tony was, as they all knew, a real family man. Nevertheless, there was always a noticeable diminution in his ebullience when Mrs. Martinelli was on the scene.

"Elsie tells me that Harry is turning up in time for eats," Ben said. For men of his—and Tony's—party, there was only one Harry. Getting a crack at him before the convention was always a plus.

Tony brightened, but he was still not himself. "Well, maybe these damned mosquitoes will start biting him, not me."

Now Elsie was a gardener, not a zealot. Hanging discreetly from trees, tentpoles and lattices, were powerful installations which electrocute insect pests in their thousands. Tony's discomfort did not spring from external causes.

"Tony! There you are!" cried Dolores, threading her way to their table. She waved Ben and Val back to their seats. "I've been looking all over for you. Come and see Elsie's calendulas."

"Sweetie," said Tony, "I don't want to see Elsie's calendulas. Sit down and take a load off your feet and I'll get you a drink."

Mrs. Martinelli was petite and amiable. "Well, if you put it that way," she said, dimpling.

This domestic vignette prompted Ben to wonder why all politicians' wives ended up sounding like Southern belles. It spurred Val to further heights.

"Dolores," he said jovially. "I don't know how you managed to get Tony to turn up at this shindig."

"Manage?" she asked, with a play of improbable eyelashes. "Why, we both love Elsie's garden!"

"Tony?" Val asked incredulously.

Tony merely closed his eyes. Dolores, however, defended him. "Tony's crazy about flowers."

She could see they were not convinced, so she added, "Just last year Tony planted two hundred and forty tulip bulbs at home!"

Apart from the conversation of several hundred voices, a strolling guitarist and the din associated with starting up the huge grill, you could have heard a pin drop. Then Val summed up.

"And they say that truth isn't stranger than fiction!"

CHAPTER 15

The whole point of a democracy is that you can go to your congressman when you want government action. Simple as this sounds, there are different ways to do it. You can throw yourself on his mercy. You can sweet talk him. You can bribe him. You can blackmail him. You can threaten his safety, his family and his political future. Naturally, circumstances will affect your selection. You're going to sound more confident if you are a union leader with thirty thousand votes in your pocket than if you are a solitary veteran complaining about a late check for GI Bill benefits.

But no matter who you are, you still have to talk to the man. That was why, a week after Elsie Hollenbach's party, Ben was anticipating word from Dean Kennison. Cautious inquiry of Ohio's two senators revealed that they, too, were waiting.

"Heisse warned me what to expect," growled Theodore Cruft. "And if Kennison wants to play politics, this is where he has to start. As a matter of fact, I've been getting ready for him. Say, Ben, did you know that the life of a radioactive isotope is . . ."

There was no doubt that wherever he surfaced, the Dean would receive a respectful hearing. He might pretend to be operating as an individual; he would be treated as the spokesman for hundreds of scientists.

By the end of the second week, Ohio's delegation had just about decided that either Humphrey Kennison had changed his mind or his intentions had been garbled in transmission. Therefore, the opening gun in Kennison's campaign caught them completely off guard. Ben, in fact, was practically naked.

After a grueling day in committee, he had made one of his infrequent visits to the House Gymnasium. He was back in the dressing room with his pants pulled on, just making the discovery that the heel of a sock had evaporated, when he was hailed.

"Hey, Ben!" came the unmistakable accents of Walter Bullivant, the Democratic Whip, "isn't this your district?"

His wet feet slapping on the floor, Ben trudged to the doorway to find all eyes riveted on the television set. United Broadcasting was twenty minutes into its evening network news. It had already covered economic indicators (good), the situation in the Middle East (bad) and the fiscal crisis in New York City (never-ending). Now it was getting to its News that Makes the News. A view of the town green in Murren was dissolving, to be succeeded by a shot of bustling downtown Newburg.

". . . ask not for whom the bell tolls. It tolls for thee," the announcer was intoning. "Every small town in America could be Murren, every city could be Newburg. Given the universality of this problem, UBC will devote a portion of its newscast every day this week to the conflict now engulfing this fertile and sleepy corner of southern Ohio—a conflict that has already claimed one life. Tonight we will examine the passions that have been aroused, and tomorrow we will show how those passions exploded into the murder of an Atomic Energy Commission official. On Wednesday we shall meet the local leaders of various factions and Thursday will be reserved for an examination in depth of the issues involved. In conclusion, on—"

"For Christ's sake," snorted someone. "They're giving this as much coverage as a moon landing."

"Ssh!"

The announcer was concluding his opening remarks. "And UBC is proud to announce that, assisting in our last three segments, will be Dr. Humphrey Kennison, the world renowned authority on hydrodynamics."

Ben felt as if he had been punched in the belly. "So that's what he's been up to," he said to himself, using a corner of the towel draped around his neck to catch water dripping from his ear. "Well, he sure hasn't been wasting any time."

An hour later, Ben had watched the program, finished dressing, received commiseration and was back in his office. Considering

the speed of Washington tom-toms he was not surprised to find
that two senators had materialized from nowhere.

Senator Gammler threatened to send them off on a side issue.

"What do they mean by a sleepy corner of Ohio?" he
demanded. "Do you think they've ever seen Cincinnati?"

Senator Cruft came from Cleveland. "Never mind that," he
barked. "What do you think that bastard Kennison wants?"

"It's as plain as the nose on your face," Ben said impatiently.
"By the time he sets foot in your office, he'll have a constituency
of millions."

"He will if this thing goes over," countered Cruft. "Half of
these explorations in depth die with a damp fizzle."

Ben thoughtfully reviewed UBC's initial performance. There
was no denying that it had been done well. Almost all the stereo-
types had been avoided. True, Murren had been shown as small
and insular, but it was. The views of Newburg, on the other
hand, had shown the changing shifts at the tire factory and the
rush-hour traffic out to the suburbs. Four vignettes had been
well-balanced. Murren got its shots with an unemployed construction worker and a retired couple living on Social Security.
The worker was running out of benefits and the couple could
not afford their property taxes. But Newburg had produced a
widow of a man who had succumbed to the aftereffects of vinyl
chloride and the father of an asthmatic child. Whatever else
UBC might be doing, it was not offering pat solutions. Instead, it
was isolating, strand by strand, the intricate network of interests
vitally affected by Buckeye Atomic.

"I doubt if this one will. It's too good," Ben said finally. "But
I'd still like to know how Kennison got them to do it."

Actually, the shoe was on the other foot. United Broadcasting
had been pursuing Humphrey Kennison for almost a year—in
fact, ever since CBS had startled the whole television world—not
least of all, itself—with a two-hour special on the Federal
Reserve System. An Emmy was one thing, but ratings higher
than a football game were enough to give any sponsor ideas.
What if the American public harbored an uncontrollable lust for
instruction? To an industry already scheduling more spinoffs of
old sitcoms, this was an alarming prognosis. Most media executives found it unwelcome.

But James Proctor, UBC's answer to Walter Cronkite, realized his moment had come. For years he had wanted to do a special entitled, "Waters of the World." He wanted to show the polluted Connecticut and the unpolluted Columbia, he wanted to show TVA and the Suez Canal, he wanted to show the arctic ice pack, he wanted . . .

In the face of all this enthusiasm UBC had been adamant. If he could get access to some of the more exotic waters of the world, if he could get an expert with recognition value, then and only then could he do his special. And as soon as James Proctor started to look for dams in Afghanistan, he came across Dean Humphrey Kennison. At first Kennison had been a harder nut to crack than the network. But now the two of them found they could help each other. So James Proctor was breaking his back to make Dean Kennison a household name.

The events of Tuesday night were a big assist. At the time, Ben Safford did not realize that he was witnessing the birth of a *cause célèbre*. The leg men of UBC had assiduously combed Murren and their industry had been rewarded. They had discovered not one, but two, home-movie records of voters' night in Murren and the disturbances that culminated in Davis Quentin's murder. UBC viewers saw flickering amateurish clips of Jonathan Fewling's charge on the flagpole, of Reverend Baines saying something from the porch steps, of a drugstore window suddenly shattering. Then James Proctor returned, gravely recounting the discovery of Quentin's body and bringing the evening's segment to a close.

But the fun had just begun. All things considered, the State Police of Ohio behaved admirably. They, too, had spent days in Murren and nobody had told them about the camera buffs. But they didn't pretend to have the magnetic pull of a big television network. They sent a polite request for copies to James Proctor. The FBI did not display the same moderation. They descended on the offices of UBC with a demand that the film be surrendered forthwith and with unspecified menaces about the obstruction of justice. United Broadcasting instantly issued a statement about the harassment of the press by federal authorities. On Wednesday morning, there were stories in the New York, Washington, St. Louis and San Francisco papers. On Wednesday afternoon, the FBI went to court to seek a writ. On Thursday morning there were editorials from coast to coast on the need for a free press.

None of this free publicity did James Proctor's series any harm. Dean Humphrey Kennison had the good fortune to make his television debut on Wednesday evening. He appeared modestly enough after Roger Gladstone had waxed enthusiastic about the potential of nuclear power, Paul Carr had sounded a vehement warning about the dangers of contamination and Sheridan Ireland had been surprisingly attractive on the need for new energy souces. Kennison achieved a small miracle by being comprehensible on the subject of waste disposal.

His big hit was on Thursday night. By that time, thanks to an ever-alert press, James Proctor was outdrawing the other three networks combined. He had promised his audience an exploration in depth of the issues, but the form that exploration took came as a blockbuster to Ben Safford and to most of Newburg County. The panel of two consisted of Kennison and Mrs. Lorraine Westerfeld. For the occasion, Dean Kennison had ceased to be a famous scientist and became a humanitarian concerned with the day-to-day needs of his community. As for Mrs. Westerfeld, she freely confided to the nation that she did not understand technical details.

"But I run a filling station," she explained, "and every day I see what my tow truck scrapes up from the accidents on the Tristate Pike. We've all learned to live with the danger of the thruway. We've decided that it's worth it. So there's no point in telling me that Buckeye Atomic will be dangerous. I expect it to be. What I really want to know is how dangerous, and what I'm getting for it."

Kennison's handsome head nodded agreement. "Exactly. It's all a question of balancing needs. There's only one thing I'd add. It's not enough to know how dangerous. Even if the danger were very small, I would still want to know if it's humanly possible to reduce the danger. I think that's one of the responsibilities of the technician. To use your own example of the car. It's up to the individual to decide if he'll accept the perils of being on the road. But it's up to Detroit to turn out as safe a car as they can."

Lorraine seemed to be enjoying her hour in the limelight. "I always say that you can't expect life to be too easy. And not just because things don't work that way. But because you lose out that way. Good heavens, plenty of people were scared of electricity in the beginning. And it can be dangerous. But think where we'd be, if nobody had been allowed to build a generator. We'd never have learned to control it."

"Fire, too, when you come to think of it."

Mrs. Wesertfeld was startled at Dean Kennison's flight of fancy.

"Well, we've had fire a long time," she said doubtfully.

"So long that it's hard to imagine any kind of life without it, but with all our experience we still need fire departments in every town and fire insurance on every house. At first it must have been absolutely terrifying. However, to use your words, mankind decided that the danger was worthwhile."

Lorraine was finding it much easier to talk to this expert than she had expected. She said so frankly.

"What's more," she continued warmly, "I can understand what you say." Her simple pleasure was an indictment of the high-powered witnesses whom Paul Carr had called in his ill-fated trial.

Kennison beamed at her. "Don't let me get started on my hob-byhorse," he warned. "The way I see it, a scientist's business isn't to tell the world what it should or should not do. He doesn't know better than everyone else. Of course, he has a right to his opinion like any ordinary man. But his job is to give people all the available information, so they can make up their own minds intelligently. And to do that, he's got to be understandable."

All through his speech, Lorraine had been bobbing her head like a Mandarin. It was high time, she thought, for this to be said.

She was very earnest when she replied. "That's all we've ever wanted in Murren. After all, if something goes wrong at Buck-eye, we'll be the first ones to feel it. We don't want poisoned water or poisoned air any more than the folks in Newburg. But we do expect to live in the twentieth century. And that seems to mean that we have to put up with an oil refinery or a gas line that could leak or a nuclear reactor. If the reactor isn't any worse than the others, then we'll go along with it. Even if the trout don't like it!"

"Everything costs something. So long as the water stays safe for human beings, I'll give you the trout." He smiled at her enthusiasm. "You could say that you and I are symbols here tonight, Mrs. Westerfeld. I'm the one who gets together all the facts and figures about reactor performance over the last twenty years, and comes up with a projection of what it should be possible to accomplish today. You're the one who has to put together the human equation and decide how that projection fits into it."

Lorraine Westerfeld's eyes were sparkling. "You could call it a partnership," she said. "I like the sound of that."

She wasn't the only one. Most of her viewers felt the same way. The program was barely off the air before the telegrams and phone calls began pouring into James Proctor's office. The audience had seen two people, very different in background and importance, but alike in several fundamentals. They both accepted the burdens of life while remaining cautiously optimistic. Dean Kennison was no Dr. Strangelove, yearning to set off bigger and better bangs. On the other hand, he did not think that the first step in cleaning up industrial pollution was to throw a whole town out of work. Mrs. Westerfeld was adult enough to recognize that certain things were too dangerous for anyone to have. But she refused to be frightened off by labels. She had to be shown. On the whole, America thought that Dean Kennison could be trusted to be impartial and Lorraine could be trusted to be sensible. Separately they were respectworthy; together they were irresistible.

James Proctor took one look at the first hour's reaction and knew that he had a winner.

"They'll be talking about them all over the country," he predicted happily.

CHAPTER 16

Naturally, the place they talked the most was Newburg, Ohio.

"Did you see Lorraine last night?" Janet, who never babbled on the phone, was perilously close to it on Friday morning.

Still going through the morning mail, Ben absently agreed that he had.

Today Janet was not satisfied with perfunctory replies. "Well, would you ever have believed it? That she could carry off something like that? Lorraine, of all people! Why, she's barely been out of Murren."

"She looked the way she always does to me," Ben confessed.

"She wasn't doing what she always does. There she was, talking to a world famous expert as if it was the kind of thing she did every day. What's more," said Janet reaching for conclusive evidence, "the network's called her to say that fan mail is piling up for her. Did you ever think Lorraine would be a big personality?"

By this time Ben was ready to admit that he had underestimated Mrs. Westerfeld's impact. "I wasn't really watching her. I was too busy keeping an eye on Kennison. He's ringing a different change every time out. God knows what he'll pull today."

"Tonight will be all technical," his sister said instantly. "James Proctor figures that enough interest has been generated so that they can get down to the nitty-gritty. He's taped a solid fifteen minutes of Kennison with some of his ex-students who run nuclear plants. Originally they were planning to edit it down to ten minutes. But the programs so far have been such a success, they decided to go with the extra time."

Ben stared at the phone in bafflement. He had long since accepted Janet's omniscience about Newburg and its environs. But since when had she penetrated the networks?

"Who told you all that? Have you got a bug in Proctor's office?"

"Don't be silly." Janet had never needed expensive equipment. With a ten-cent phone call she could accomplish more than the CIA with its annual budget. "Naturally I congratulated Lorraine first thing this morning, and she had it all straight from Dean Kennison last night."

"I thought they taped these things ahead of time."

"Of course they do. Lorraine had Kennison up for dinner, so they could watch themselves on television. She was afraid maybe she'd made a fool of herself, but he told her she'd done a fine job, and all those calls pouring into the studio prove that he was right."

"She sounded swell," said Ben loyally, knowing that his tribute would be passed on. "But, all the same, I was sure surprised to see her. These people on television panels usually all look alike. Proctor must have had a brainstorm when he decided to match Lorraine with a professor."

"Good heavens! It wasn't James Proctor who picked her, it was Kennison. He met all the selectmen when he was in Murren, and he decided that Lorraine and he would be naturals together."

A dim suspicion was forming in Ben's mind. Dean Humphrey Kennison seemed to be spending a good deal of time in Murren, and most of it with Mrs. Westerfeld.

"Well now the two of them have gotten together, do you think anything will come of it? Isn't Kennison a widower?"

Janet's chuckle was more of a snort than a laugh. "It's nothing like that," she said comfortably. "Lorraine tells me that he's just glad to get out of the house. You know he's staying with the Carrs, and that isn't easy these days. Paul Carr is acting worse and worse."

Ben thought back to Wednesday's telecast. "He seemed all right on the show. More reasonable than usual, as a matter of fact."

"That was for public consumption! Privately he's running around saying that Kennison should stick to his ivory tower, that Newburg already has the AEC and Tristate throwing their weight around and we don't need any more outsiders. He also has a nice line about how experts sell out to the AEC so they can get on their paid consultant list."

"No wonder Kennison wants to get out of the house," Ben sympathized. "That must be one happy family under that roof."

"I can't help feeling sorry for Abby. I ran into her at the hospital, and she broke her back trying to explain how they both assumed her father would be just as anti-Buckeye as they are. She says they're disappointed at the neutral position he's taking."

This was too much for Ben. "For God's sake! Did they think a scientist would run off at the mouth without having any of the facts?"

"Abby's just trying to save face. She's not going to admit her husband is eaten up with jealousy because her father is a star on national television. The poor little thing looked absolutely miserable, Ben. After all, if it were any other family problem, she'd get some rest from it. But no matter where she goes—the supermarket, her job, the library—nobody is talking about anything else."

From far away in the New House Office Building, Ben said, "It's only natural that everyone in town should be watching the UBC news. It's the first time Newburg has been on television."

"Good heavens! That's not what's causing the excitement. It's the fact that James Proctor is here." Janet clucked her tongue in exasperation as she sought words to describe the phenomenon. "Can you imagine what this town is like, Ben? They've been here for over two weeks now. For a start, Proctor rented the whole Colonial Motel. Gladys told me that Pete almost fainted when he took the reservation. Then you should see the equipment they brought in—closed trucks that have offices inside and open trucks with big booms and great big recording consoles. Why, the outside of the Colonial looks as if the circus has come to town. The entire police force is moonlighting for them. They had to reroute traffic for blocks when they filmed James Proctor in front of the courthouse. And, whenever he sets foot outdoors, a crowd piles up."

Dazed, Ben realized that he had been misled by his own experience with television. Now that he had racked up a respectable tenure in the House, he was sometimes on panels such as "Face the Nation" and "Meet the Press." But the excitement was limited to his appearance on the tube. The actual screening involved only a staid trip to the studio. If he had paused to think, he would have understood the implications of all those open-air shots on the Proctor newscast.

"And were you fighting for a look at the great man, too?"

"I didn't have to," Janet announced smugly. "Fred and I were in Wong's Village when he brought the whole crew in to eat Chinese."

"That figures." In England there was the Nelson touch. In Newburg it was the Janet touch. "Well, it sounds like a real Donnybrook. I'm surprised you didn't try to rope me in for it."

"I thought about it." She seemed to feel some defense was necessary. "But there was no way they could pussyfoot around Davis Quentin's murder, so I decided against it."

"Thank God!"

*   *

Other people would have given their eyeteeth to join Ben on the side lines.

"And that includes the whole damned AEC," groaned Jim Vorhees.

"Oh, come on, Jim. I thought they did a pretty good job Friday night." What Ben really meant was that he had understood what was going on. "And you can't claim that Kennison packed the panel. He had one expert who was anti nuclear power, one who was all for it and two who were sitting on the fence."

"And every one of them an ex-student," Vorhees said darkly.

"Well, what difference does that make? So long as they weren't all taking pot shots at you, I don't see what you've got to complain about."

Under pressure, Vorhees shifted ground and revealed the real grievance.

"It isn't so much what was on the series, as the way Kennison is using it. Now that he's got all this publicity, we've got to watch our step every inch of the way with him."

But Ben remembered the shivers of anticipation produced in the Newburg Courthouse when Joseph Altschuler and Charles Brandenburg had first let the cat out of the bag.

"You were going to do that anyhow, the minute Kennison appeared on the scene. Nothing's changed except that he's been a big success on Proctor's program. And you know what that amounts to. Within a week, people will forget his name."

"Like hell they will! I guess you're not clued into the scientific scuttlebutt. The word is, that he's in line for the Nobel prize. They gave it for high-yield wheat a couple of years ago. That one was for food. Now, they're just about ready for water."

All this gloom and doom was beginning to irritate Ben.

"Honest to God, I don't know what's gotten into you, Jim. The Nobel prize is peanuts compared to an appearance on the Johnny Carson show. You better decide whether you're going to fish or cut bait. If you're worried about Kennison's scientific prestige, he had all he needed long before last week. If you're worried about him as a public personality, I expect James Proctor has had his money's worth out of Kennison, and the worst is over."

Vorhees sounded more southern than ever as he drawled out the next bit of calamitous information. "You ought to keep up with these things, Ben. Particularly now that Newburg is on the map. The way I hear it, Proctor and Kennison have gone into business together. Last week was just the beginning. Proctor's planning one of those all-night specials—all about water and pollution and energy. Apparently he was having trouble on the international end until he teamed up with Kennison. Then all the tracks were cleared." For a moment Vorhees forgot his own problems as he continued in a hushed voice, "They say that all Dean Kennison did was make one phone call to Peking, and twenty-four hours later the Peoples Republic gave UBC the go-ahead to shoot footage along the Yellow River. Now that's what I call clout!"

"All you have to do is know the right person to call," Ben said. He could never understand why people who knew the ropes in Washington were stupefied to learn that things in Moscow and Cairo and Jakarta were done the same way.

"Maybe." Vorhees was unconvinced. "Or it just might be that

every Minister of Development in the whole world snaps to attention when he hears the name Humphrey Kennison. But what really matters is that Proctor isn't the only one in that industry who knows he struck it rich with Kennison. All the networks are trying to sign him up to appear on those Sunday panel shows. And he's saying yes to all comers. Your crack about Johnny Carson wasn't so far off the mark."

Ben frowned thoughtfully. "That's funny. From everything I've heard, Kennison doesn't seem to be a publicity hound. And if you're telling me this is all a build-up for his little chat with the Ohio delegation, I say you're crazy. It would be using a pile driver to crack a nut."

"Oh, it's bigger than Murren, all right. Kennison has soared beyond that. As soon as he started to look at Buckeye professionally, he saw what a lot of work there is to be done on nuclear safety. I suppose it was a natural for someone with his experience. He's always been the kind of guy who's broken new ground. Now he's trained a younger generation to take over his old work, and he's ripe for a new crusade. He says that by the time he's done, it'll be safer to have an atomic reactor in your back yard than a supermarket."

"I gather you've seen him."

"Seen him!" Vorhees almost choked. "What do you think I've been griping about? We can't get him out of our hair. He's already got the files on all operating facilities. He's breaking the list down into types of piles and kinds of safety systems. Then that gets subdivided into the boil-off and steam-off methods. Ultimately he'll be zeroing in on the coolant technology. All this is just for openers. His field trips start tomorrow. While he's gone, we're going to be pulling all our research reports for him."

If this catalogue of woe was designed to elicit sympathy, it misfired.

"You're sure giving him the whole ball of wax. Is there anything he's asked for that you haven't agreed to?"

"I haven't been the one giving him things." Suddenly Jim Vorhees sounded older and harder. "I was all for fighting every inch of the way. Oh, sure, I'm ready to co-operate with an eminent scientist. But co-operation is one thing, and abdication is another. The trouble with Andy Heisse is that he doesn't know anything about the civil service. He's just another one of these politicians running for office—"

"Oh, yes?" Ben interrupted.

"Don't get me wrong, Ben. I'm not saying you people up on the Hill don't know your business."

"Sure."

"And there's nothing wrong in running for office. It's just that . . ." Vorhees had been flustered into launching a long and useless apology before realizing its futility. Abruptly he switched tactics. "Dammit, Ben, you know what I mean. Heisse is great at protecting the Agency when it comes to infighting with the FBI and the Department of Justice. His instincts are dead right. But just the idea of network television is enough to scare him out of his pants. He sees all those voters in California turning against him, and before you know it, he's putting the whole AEC up for grabs."

Ben shook his head. "I'm not certain I do know what you mean, Jim. Here's a respectable scientist who wants to work on safety development. You say you've got nothing against it and you're willing to co-operate. Kennison's not asking for stuff that's out of line. It's all relevant technical data. So I ask myself why fight him every inch of the way?"

He did not have to add the final question he was asking. Anybody in Washington could supply it. If you're willing to fight so hard, you must be hiding something. What are you sitting on over there?

Vorhees supplied the answer anyway.

"The AEC isn't running a cover-up. No one gave Tristate its permit in return for a big fat check," he said steadily. "You forget that we've dealt with plenty of scientists. And even the ones on our payroll aren't short on integrity. Kennison's the odd man out, not me. You might ask him what he's really up to, when he gets around to you."

"What's that supposed to mean?"

"He's not planning to write a paper on coolants and publish it in the *Review of Modern Physics*. He's talking about changing procedures and relations with power companies. That's why

Heisse is such a fool to knuckle under. Kennison doesn't want to help anybody. He intends to take over the AEC—lock, stock and barrel!"

*　　　*

"Well, what if he does?" Val Oakes asked sleepily. "It could be a mighty big improvement, if you ask me."

He and Ben were idling over their dessert, reluctant to leave the air-conditioned restaurant for the first heat wave of the season.

"Are things that bad over at the AEC? You people on the Joint Committee haven't been demanding any changes." Ben assembled the remains of his strawberry shortcake in a neat pile and raised a forkful, ready to enjoy Val Oakes on the subject of committee action.

"I ask you, Ben, how in God's name can we set up a squawk? We don't know what's going on. They've got this corral of tame experts, and not one of them can talk English. And if we ever do come up with a question, they're ready and eager to help all right. They snow us with information. Stacks of it, and all in equations."

This was a familiar lament in the halls of Congress. Every agency in Washington, at one time or another, has tried to raise a shield of esoteric detail between itself and its congressional watchdog. The legislature was tolerant of this tactic at intervals. What Val Oakes was bemoaning was the chronic inability to communicate manifested by all testifying scientists.

"Even if they wanted to explain something to us, I don't think they'd know how," he summarized.

It was for that very reason, Ben observed, that Andrew Heisse had been appointed a commissioner of the AEC. Nobody had ever claimed that he was big on equations.

"But he doesn't know any more than we do. As soon as we get past the morning blessing," Val said, draining his coffee, "he has to send for someone in a laboratory."

"You mean it's a choice between evils?"

"No, I don't." Val was stirred, for him, to noteworthy enthusiasm. He was even sitting upright. "I liked the sound of Kennison when he was on Proctor's newscast. I understood every word he said. It shows it isn't impossible. If the AEC doesn't wangle him, then, by golly, maybe the Joint Committee should."

Ben did not need any more ratings. Anything that could turn both Janet and Val Oakes into partisans was home free.

CHAPTER 17

It was unfair to claim that Ben Safford had been skulking in Washington to avoid the UBC cameras. With the House still tied into knots over the President's veto of the Merchant Marine Act, with the Speaker still bird dogging Lou Flecker and the subcommittee about the National Meterological Services Bill, Ben was fully occupied and more. Only coincidence synchronized his weekend trip home with the departure of James Proctor.

"Besides," he said, jamming papers into a briefcase, "if I listened to you and Janet, I wouldn't have any voting record at all. I'd be too busy competing with Lucy re-runs."

"Don't forget to take the Fillmore resolution," Madge advised. "You said you wanted to read it again, when you had the time."

Suspecting a barb, Ben shoveled the Fillmore resolution in. "Plenty of people have made a big mistake, thinking politics is a TV game show."

"And here's Mrs. Hollenbach's comment on the subcommittee agenda for next Monday," said Madge, to show that he was making no headway.

It was an old bone of contention. Ben had appeared on the home screen more than he wanted. Enough was enough. Newburg already knew that he did not have perfect teeth, a full head of hair, and a boyish smile. There was no use rubbing it in.

"Anyway," Ben told his secretary, "the eyes of the nation may be on Newburg, but this Saturday the eyes of Newburg are on basketball."

Madge was a stalwart supporter of Ben's, but her territory was Washington. Some rites and rituals she had to take on faith.

"If you say so," she replied dubiously.

He felt that he owed her an explanation. "It's the first time the Newburg Huskies have made the semifinals of the state high school championship."

Mentally, he could see, she was pitting the Huskies against James Proctor and his millions of viewers. So Ben went on, "We're playing our traditional rivals, the Bladesville Blades."

In the last analysis, Madge was for him, not against him. "Well," she said gamely, "good luck!"

*　　　*

Back on Plainfield Road, Janet did not need convincing. "Of course it's a must for you, Ben. They sold out all six thousand seats months ago. Minnie Gormley tells me that they're installing loudspeakers in the assembly hall and the girls' gym to handle the overflow."

Ben's tastes were simple. "It sounds like a good game. Have we got decent seats, Fred?"

On Saturday afternoons, Lundgren's service shop was closed.

"Great seats," Fred replied, rummaging through his wallet. "Here's your ticket. We'll meet you there!"

"Meet me there?" Ben echoed. "Why? Are you two going out to dinner or something?"

"We're not," grinned Fred. "You are."

Before Ben could demand an explanation, Janet was giving him one. "I know it's just a flying trip, Ben, but I thought it was a good idea to line up a few things this afternoon. And Ed Daly doesn't have a free minute until dinner time. You can grab a sandwich with him. That will leave you plenty of time to get over to the high school."

A lazy do-nothing Saturday afternoon had sounded too good to be true, and it was. Janet interpreted his expression perfectly.

"There's been so much excitement about this James Proctor series," she explained. "It can't do you any harm to start taking some soundings. Everybody involved with Buckeye has been talking his head off. What you need are some outside views."

"Just in case?" Ben asked.

She was quite firm. "Just in case."

Ben knew she was right, so he was more fatalistic than bitter.

"Okay, Janet. But tell me, am I giving any speeches before the game?"

"Don't tempt her," said Fred.

Janet had some more good advice. "Try to get to the field house early enough to shake some hands," she said. "And for heaven's sake, drive carefully."

"Janet," said her brother, "take your choice."

Ben set out in one of Fred's Fords, driving so carefully that he was ten minutes late at Rudy Wiersma's downtown office. Fortunately Rudy was a fast talker.

"Glad to see you, Ben, glad to see you. Jan said you were coming home to catch the big one. Say, it's going to be some game, isn't it? You know Rudy Junior is in the starting line-up?"

Ben didn't know, but he said the right thing anyway.

"Yeah," said Rudy. "If he works as hard as he practices dribbling, the kid's going to make a million. Listen, Ben, the reason I wanted to talk with you . . ."

Rudy was a union man as well as a father. Since Local 605, International Brotherhood of Electricians, came out strong for Ben every other November, they had his ear whenever they wanted it.

"What's with this TV blitz?" Wiersma wanted to know. "I'm getting calls from the guys. Are the jobs certain, or is there any chance of somebody still pulling the rug out?"

Ben was halfway into his next sentence before Rudy's words sank in. "Jobs?" he said. "Nobody's started hiring yet."

"Don't kid yourself," said Rudy. "Trage's hired thirteen— count 'em, thirteen—electricians. And I understand Wendgraf Construction is taking on carpenters. I happen to know that Van Lawlor has put five new plumbers on his payroll. No, Ben, Tristate's not going on TV and blabbing about it, and the subs aren't spilling the beans. But they're pushing right ahead with Buckeye. What I want to know . . ."

Since Buckeye was still a long way from the halls of Congress, Ben escaped without any binding commitments. Nevertheless, he was thoughtful and, as the afternoon progressed, he began picking up more hints.

Norm DeLuria was chairman of the Real Estate Board.

". . . so I said to Janet, ask Ben to drop in," he said with a salesman's smile that happened to be perfectly genuine. "Seeing as how you were coming home for the big game."

Memory stirred and Ben recalled that DeLuria had been All-State at Newburg High and All-Star at Bowling Green. He knew what to ask. Was Norm Junior playing?

"Four girls," said Norm sadly. "Ben, do you know something I don't?"

"Along what lines?" Ben temporized, although he could guess what was coming.

"Buckeye! I've been watching Proctor just like everybody else. So it's a big debate. But the way I figure it, that's just to keep the natives quiet. What the hell is happening out there in Murren?"

"You tell me," said Ben.

When Buckeye was first announced, some real estate activity had been sparked in Murren. But delay, controversy—and, perhaps, murder—had put a lid on it. Now, even while James Proctor was exploring the problem in depth, unnamed buyers were moving in, gobbling up farms and pastures, talking options and subdivisions.

"I like to see people make money," said DeLuria. "Hell, I've handled a couple of sales myself. But I want to know what's up."

"George Barry?" Ben suggested, recalling something Janet had said.

Norm laughed aloud. "Old George is in there trying, all right. But he's nickel-and-dime stuff. This is big shots from out of town, and they're spending in a big way. I figure they're insiders —maybe Tristate, maybe Lomax. But does that mean the whole fight is over?"

"Not according to what I see on TV," said Ben. "But I'll be asking around."

His last port of call was the man who had the answers. Ed Daly was chairman of the County Democratic Party. Over a roast beef sandwich at Cronin's, opposite the courthouse, he said,

"No, I'm not going to the basketball game. Why should I?"

Offhand, Ben could not think of a single good reason. "How are things, Ed?"

Daly always fleshed out Janet's progress reports in some detail. Between soybean prices and the funding for the school lunch program, he did not reach Buckeye until it was almost time for Ben to leave.

". . . a lot of coverage. Still, the Republicans are lying low, Ben. From here, it doesn't look to me as if it's going to be a big party issue. Sure, you may have lost a few votes in Lincolnwood. But it hasn't hurt you in the city."

Ben appreciated this single-minded approach and said so. He then asked what was going on.

"What do you think?" Ed asked rhetorically. "Sherry Ireland and Tristate are trying to beat the gun. They've got their permit. If they can get the thing up, the battle is over—no matter how much hot air the other side produces. It doesn't pay to underestimate bricks and mortar, either."

"And I hear they're already hiring," said Ben.

"Sure they are," said Daly. "And I've got some friends over at the Teamsters. Hell, the whole reactor that everybody's kicking up such a stink about is already here in Newburg—in pieces. Trucks have been hauling loads from Lomax for over a week now."

The land boom came as news to him, but no surprise. "That's how it goes. By now, half of Sherry Ireland's staff is trying to cash in. Or it's the old bastard himself. Say, Ben, you'd better get going. The time to put in an appearance is before the game starts."

"Great minds work alike," said Ben rising. "So, nobody thinks Kennison's got a chance of stopping Buckeye, despite all this ink he's been getting."

Daly was a born handicapper. If it hadn't been politics, it would have been horses. "Nobody in this neck of the woods," he told Ben. "And between you and me, if they thought he did, they'd find a way of stopping him. So long, Ben, I'll give you a ring tomorrow."

The Newburg High School Field House came as a refreshing change from the smoke-filled room that Ed Daly carried around with him. A vast cheerful mob was funnelling past the ticket takers, exhilarated by the songs and cheers that wafted tantalizingly out of the auditorium.

"Give me a K, a K, a K!"

"With Newburg in tri-umph flashing . . ."

It gave a whole new meaning to pressing the flesh, thought Ben as the body weight of his constituents churned him onward. Whether he was headed in the right direction was an open question.

"Hey there, Ben!"

"Nice to see you, Doc!"

"Mr. Safford . . ."

What handshaking he managed was at shoulder level, over intervening heads, so that a good many of the people Janet and Ed wanted him to see were wedged into his armpit.

"I beg your pardon, Mrs. Strottle. Oh, is this Billy? Grown so much I wouldn't have recognized him."

The tide finally deposited him at the foot of the stairs to the balcony. Here Ben struggled into a corner and tried to take stock. Row E, Seat 18, the stub read. Now where the hell . . . ?

"Ben!"

There was no mistaking this ebullient greeting.

"Hello, Lorraine," said Ben, finally locating her. "I see you're not high-hatting your old friends, now that you're a TV celebrity. How's your fan mail?"

"Just as good as Humphrey's," she replied in high spirits. "Isn't it, Humphrey?"

Catching sight of her two companions, Ben realized he had fetched up in the middle of Buckeye again. Not that Dean Kennison looked as if he were thinking about atomic energy. Beaming with unalloyed enjoyment, he said, "I've just got back from a little trip to Urbana and into Kentucky. And the only thing people ask me is what Mrs. Westerfeld is really like!"

"Oh, go on!"

A smashing personal success can be a heady experience. Ben understood the overflowing satisfaction lapping both Lorraine and Kennison. But so, it developed, did Roger Gladstone.

"The trouble with you two is that you've become show biz types, and there's no holding you down. Safford, would you believe that some kid just asked for Lorraine's autograph?"

This joshing did not convince Ben that Ping-pong diplomacy works. He still doubted if the Huskies-Blades epic had turned adversaries into friends. It would take more than a basketball game to influence Kennison. And, if Roger Gladstone was helping Ireland sneak Buckeye under Kennison's nose, what better camouflage than good-natured ribbing?

But if that was the case, the camouflage was wearing a little thin.

"Did I hear you say you're just here for a few days, Humphrey?" Gladstone asked with more than casual interest.

"That's right," Kennison told him with a quizzical light in his eye. "I'm on my rounds tomorrow."

"Oh?" said Gladstone.

Kennison was savoring his advantage. "Yes," he said. Only after a marked interval did he expand. "After I see a few people in Indianapolis, I'm on my way up to Michigan, Roger."

"I can think of more interesting itineraries," said Gladstone, with a laugh.

But Ben had caught the crosscurrent between the two men, and so had Lorraine. Tonight, she was out for fun.

"Anyway, when Humphrey called up, I told him he really ought to come to the game. Lincolnwood isn't giving him a fair picture of Newburg—that's what I say. Don't you agree, Ben?"

Ben was not poormouthing any part of the Ohio Fiftieth, but, as Ed Daly had reminded him, Lincolnwood was not Safford country.

"All this"—he winced as he was elbowed from behind—"sure is a pretty good way to get to know Newburg." Then, since his antennae told him that Lincolnwood, and by extension Paul and Abby Carr, might lead him out of his depth, he turned to Gladstone. "What brings you here?"

Gladstone had been woolgathering. "You mean the basketball game? Hell, when I'm out on a job, I get sick of spending my evenings in motel rooms. I take in as many of these events as I can find. Even bingo games."

"You were lucky to be able to get a ticket," said Ben.

With a wink at Lorraine, Gladstone said, "George Barry gave me his."

"Why, that means you're sitting with us!" she exclaimed, not altogether concealing her dismay.

But Humphrey Kennison did not seem to mind. "Doing a lot of hard work, Roger?" he asked. "I approve of that. You can't overdo."

Gladstone was elaborately casual. "Just the usual last-minute details, before we get rolling, Humphrey. You know how it is."

"I know," said Kennison blandly.

Lorraine was bursting to ask them what they were talking about but fortunately a great roar suddenly shook the air. "My goodness," she yipped, tugging on Kennison's sleeve. "The game's begun!"

But it was only the Huskies coming out onto the court. However, when Ben finally located Row E, the game did begin. During its action-packed opening minutes, he was helplessly passing knee after knee to get to Seat 18.

"Down in front!"

"There you are!" said Janet when he finally made it to her side. "Quick, sit down!"

"Where?"

Ben was not only blocking the view of some of his constituents, he was squeezing the rest into the aisle.

"And the Blades have already made two quick baskets," Fred told him dolefully. "Here, want a chicken leg?"

Despite the comfort of Janet's wicker basket, despite the frenzy of the cheerleaders, it was a sorrowful first half for Newburg. At the buzzer, the band broke loose, and so did disheartened fans.

"Considering the athletic department's budget . . ."

"Why did he leave that Waner kid in?"

"A sixteen-point lead!"

Suddenly, the announcer cut in on the Bladesville band which was outdoing itself.

". . . to welcome friends and visitors to Newburgh High and introduce a few folks who are here tonight. Mayor Wilhelm . . ."

Four rows down, His Honor stood up, waved energetically, then sat down to a good hand.

". . . and Congressman Safford. Take a bow, Ben!"

They caught him with his mouth full, but tonight not even rock-ribbed Republicans could hold that against him.

". . . and the gal the whole country has been watching, our own Lorraine Westerfeld. Stand up, Lorraine! Where are you? There she is, folks!"

High in the balcony Lorraine rose to a tremendous ovation. She blew kisses, dithered, then hauled Humphrey Kennison to his feet. The ovation continued.

"Ed Daly may have been wrong," Ben mused.

"What was that?" Janet asked.

"I'll tell you later."

"Well, I'll tell you one thing right now," said Janet. "It's a good thing the Carrs aren't here tonight. They wouldn't understand this, at all."

Ben was not altogether sure that he did, either.

CHAPTER 18

But, as the days passed, nobody had difficulty understanding how Dean Humphrey Kennison had bulldozed through all those flood-control dams, hydroelectric generators and irrigation systems. The Dean was a glutton for work, tirelessly jetting from one installation to another, while his directives, memorandums, and requests bombarded desks in every corner of the Atomic Energy Commission. It was not a question of superhuman powers. The School of Engineering at Midwestern University contained one secretary, two research assistants and an associate dean who had transformed Kennison's office into Mission Control. Kennison stayed on top of all this activity by utilizing every stray moment to prop himself up in a public booth, to commandeer the motel switchboard or to lean across the desk and borrow his host's phone.

"Now listen, Beatrice, this is what I want you to do," he would say, flipping the pages of his little notebook. "Drop a line to the librarian at the AEC, thanking him for the material he sent last week and asking him for the '66 reports. Have Luke finish his comparison of the water-jacket systems. Set it up as a memo from me to the people at R&D in Washington, with copies to the field stations in Santa Rosa and Greensville. Wait a minute! You'd better add Professor Kenneth Maddigan at Carnegie Tech to our general distribution list. And give Joe Altschuler a ring, will you? Tell him I'll be landing in Indianapolis tomorrow on Flight 93, and I'll come straight to his office."

Some secretaries would have collapsed under this treatment but Beatrice, casually scrawling pothooks on her stenographic pad,

had been hardened by years of bad connections with Quito and
garbled cables from Mombasa. By the time Kennison called the
next morning with fresh orders, she was able to report that the
backlog had been cleared up and a long-awaited letter from
Egypt had arrived.

"Good!" said Kennison, who derived fresh vigor from every
ball added to his juggling routine. "Then get hold of Proctor
over at UBC and tell him he's got his go-ahead for the Aswan
Dam. If he wants to talk to me about it, tonight is out. Tell him
to try me Thursday in Lexington. Let's see, I'll be at . . ."

There was a sound of riffling that Beatrice interpreted cor-
rectly. "I've got you a room at the Olde Kentucky Inn," she
forestalled him. "I'll tell him you're usually in by ten."

"And remind him that he's inviting Heisse and Congressman
Safford to join that panel." Kennison chuckled genially. "That
should make them sit up and take notice."

He could afford to chuckle. While his opponents—both actual
and potential—were being diverted by swarms of gnats, he was
free to zero in on his own target. By the time that the AEC
stopped worrying about fishing expeditions in its files, by the
time that Senator Cruft (R., Ohio) stopped worrying about what
position Congressman Safford (D., Ohio) would take, he would
have perfected a program for ensuring optimum safety standards
at nuclear energy plants. As far as Humphrey Kennison was concerned, that was the hard part. Once the program was formulated, he never doubted his ability to ram it home.

In the end he outstripped his own timetable. Long before his
victims were considering a counterattack, he was once again on
the phone. But now he was bypassing Mission Control and talking directly to Roger Gladstone.

". . . didn't expect to come up with anything this soon," he
said, still surprised by his own speed. "Now, I don't say this
solves the central problem, but every step forward is something
accomplished."

"You don't think maybe you're going too fast, Humphrey?"
Gladstone was doing his best to be tactful. "I know you're under pressure to come up with some results fast, but you haven't
been on the job very long—"

The attempt was unsuccessful.

"Pressure has nothing to do with it," Kennison said stiffly. "It's my plain duty to keep the AEC apprised of my work as I go along. That way, when I present final proposals, they'll be in a position to evaluate them."

"All right, all right," Gladstone muttered, wishing that Kennison would come down off his high horse and forget that he was a college professor.

"I intend to call Washington and ask for a conference tomorrow. Naturally I assumed that you'd wish to take part, and support me. But if you'd rather not be present, that's your decision."

Many an African official would have recognized the are-you-with-me-or-against-me ultimatum. It had brought most of them to their knees and it did not fail now.

"Oh, I'll be there. Just tell me what time."

Gladstone sounded very tired, but he knew he was going to have company before the day was out.

*   *

"I'm sorry to interrupt." Jim Vorhees' apology was perfunctory as he poked his head around the door to the commissioner's office.

Andrew Heisse looked up from his conversation. "Can't it wait? Nina and I just got back from HEW, and I want to go over these new guidelines with her."

"Not if you want to keep your friend Kennison sweet, it can't wait."

Heisse flushed. "He's not particularly my friend. But I'm realistic enough to move with the times. The trouble with you, Jim, is you can't see that Kennison with his big TV following is just as important to the AEC's future as Senator Blaney."

"Senator Blaney has been head of the Joint Committee a long time, and he doesn't throw his weight around this way," Vorhees retorted.

Thus far Nina Yeager had been content to follow the exchange, her smooth head cocked to one side. But she was not diffident when she joined in.

"I don't see that we have anything to complain about," she said judiciously. "After all, Jim, at first you expected Kennison to be dead against our generators and he hasn't taken a hard and fast line. He's simply asked for a chance to evaluate the work done to date."

Jim Vorhees was too worked up to settle into a chair. He was striding back and forth across Heisse's large corner room, his hands jammed inside his pockets. "You haven't been around here as long as I have, Nina," he flung over his shoulder. "I've seen the detached-scientist act before. It's the way they mask the fact that they're just as opinionated as everybody else."

"Some of them, maybe. But you've forgotten all the material Dean Kennison has borrowed from our archives. He's planning a real study."

"Ha!" Vorhees laughed sardonically. "A fat chance we've got of a real study when he starts acting up within a couple of weeks. I grant you he's better at window dressing than most of them."

"I don't believe it," Nina said stubbornly. "If we had the right kind of operation, we wouldn't have to run scared every time somebody wants to look at our files."

"You know better than that. If somebody's out to get you—"

"Just a minute!" Heisse's decisive tone quelled his subordinates. When they both fell silent, he continued, "You still haven't explained why you came charging in here, Jim. Exactly how is Kennison acting up?"

Vorhees' reply was delivered so slowly and evenly that it was a parody of self-control. "He really wanted to talk to you, but the matter is so urgent he was willing to settle for me. We're to arrange a meeting for tomorrow so that he can present an interim progress report. He's already decided on the time and place and some of the participants. You're to drop everything and be there at two o'clock, I'm to be there and Gladstone has agreed to come. He didn't tell me whether he's invited the television cameras."

Heisse ignored the petulance of the speech. "I didn't expect him to get back to us this soon," he admitted worriedly. "What's gotten him so excited that we have to have a summit conference?"

"I don't know. I didn't see that it made any difference," Vorhees replied in long-suffering tones guaranteed to goad the other. "Under our new ground rules, what Kennison wants, Kennison gets."

"For Christ's sake!" Heisse exploded. "You mean you didn't even ask him?"

"Of course I asked him!" Vorhees snapped back. "And he had the nerve to tell me that he'd rather not have misleading summaries leaking from our offices. When he got here, he'd be able to put everything in proper context."

Heisse did not share Jim Vorhees' sense of affront. "Well, we have had a lot of leaks," he said absently while his brow wrinkled in thought. "Still, it's odd, damned odd."

*   *

The oddity was soon spreading to Newburg, Ohio. When Paul Carr returned from lunch he found a message slip on his desk spike that made him stare blankly. Then he plunged out to the secretary he shared with two other juniors.

"What's all this supposed to be about?" he demanded, shaking the pink form so vigorously she could not possibly read it.

But Mrs. Merton was approximately thirty years older than he was and had spent most of that time interval in law offices. She calmly plucked the offending paper from his grasp and scrutinized it.

"It means what it says. Dr. Humphrey Kennison called and asked you to join him at an AEC meeting in Washington tomorrow afternoon."

"How come? Is he still on that UBC kick, or is this about Murren?" The questions came tumbling over each other. "What does he want me for?"

"You know as much as I do," Mrs. Merton said cheerfully.

Paul sighed heavily. "Then you'd better get him back. I'll have to straighten this out myself."

But Mrs. Merton was way ahead of him. "I thought of that, so I asked for his number. He was checking out of his motel to go to the airport."

"Just like him," Paul muttered ungraciously. Stymied, he continued to pore over the two short sentences that had come in at one o'clock. "I suppose he might have talked to Abby. I could call her," he argued to himself.

Mrs. Merton's finger was hovering over the dial when he suddenly changed his mind. "Never mind about that. I'll speak to my wife later. Right now get me the legal department at the AEC. I want Attorney Nina Yeager."

It was the first time that he had dared contact Nina in her office. But the mounting frustration of the past two weeks was taking its toll. Paul Carr was tired of being swept aside from the main action. There had been a certain satisfaction in his public performances at Murren and at Tristate's colloquium, a certain thrill in trying his first court case. But it had been downhill all the way, ever since the jury found against him. Or, as an inner voice told him, ever since Humphrey Kennison had taken over. If his father-in-law simply wanted him to form part of an admiring audience, then he'd be damned if he would go to Washington. And Nina was the only person likely to tell him.

But, when reached, she was a disappointment.

"I don't know what all the excitement is about," she complained. "Everybody here is in a flap, but no one will admit they know what's going on. Of course, Jim Vorhees was the one who actually spoke to Dean Kennison, and ordinarily I wouldn't put it past Jim to keep something up his sleeve."

"Then get it out of him!"

"I'm willing to bet that he's not playing games this time. You see, Sherry Ireland from Tristate just blew in, breathing fire and brimstone. He's been in town for the past few days and his invitation was forwarded from Cincinnati. Apparently Dean Kennison wouldn't give them any idea about the meeting, either."

"Dammit, I've got to find out," Carr insisted. "I'm not going to play patsy to the great man sounding off about the future of nuclear safety."

At her desk, Nina was even brusquer than in her living room. "Try using what brains you've got," she advised. "Honestly, Paul, whenever your father-in-law is the issue, you stop thinking straight and go completely haywire."

There was a long pause.

"Do you have anything specific in mind?" he finally grated. "Or is this just Nancy Drew, girl lawyer, talking?"

She was impatient with his obtuseness.

"For heaven's sake! When he invites Sherry Ireland and Roger

Gladstone to a meeting, Kennison isn't going to be talking about universals. He's going to be talking about Buckeye Atomic!"

*　*

For all his bluster, Sheridan Ireland was capable of reasoning his way from A to B. He had already arrived at the same conclusion as Nina Yeager, and was taking his own precautions.

". . . and I call it disgraceful," he was saying to the phone, "that when the AEC is having a meeting about Buckeye Atomic, they should invite everyone except those most nearly affected by any decision taken. I refer, of course, to the good people of Murren."

George Barry was not as skilled in picking up cues as most of Ireland's associates.

"I guess those big shots in Washington think they can get away with anything," he said, struggling valiantly.

Ireland could see that he would have to be more explicit. "If, for some reason like dirty politics, certain groups were trying to get the AEC to cancel its approval for Buckeye, they would naturally make their move in a closed meeting where the public wouldn't know what they were up to."

"You mean they're going to shaft us?" Barry squawked in dismay. "You can't let them do that, Mr. Ireland."

Ireland no longer expected Barry to make his suggestion for him.

"I propose to turn their secret caucus into an open meeting," he throbbed with enough volume to fill a hall. "No decision is going to be made in the absence of the selectmen of Murren. I would be grateful, *very* grateful, if you would join me at my hotel tomorrow before the meeting. We can plan our tactics before we go over to the AEC together."

George Barry was dazzled at the vision of himself as a wheeler-dealer in the nation's capital.

"You can count on me, Mr. Ireland," he said fervently. "I'll tell it to them the way it is."

*　*

But radiant visions of self have no value unless they are shared.

"So he said to me, George, we're all relying on you to put together a plan that's in the best interests of Murren."

Lorraine Westerfeld was a kind-hearted woman who believed in being on good terms with her neighbors.

"That sounds swell, George."

"And then he wanted me to be in Washington with him. Of course, it's not easy for me to leave the business, but I thought it was my duty."

This part was new to Lorraine but still she nodded amiably.

"After all, we don't want those bureaucrats making any final decision without getting the views of the town selectmen."

But his boasting had led him too far.

"That's funny," mused Lorraine rubbing the end of her nose reflectively. "If Ireland wants to get any punch out of the views of Murren's selectmen, you'd think he'd have asked for them formally. You could have taken a resolution, or some such, to Washington with you."

"Well, he doesn't know how this meeting is going to go. Hell, Lorraine, he isn't even sure why Kennison called it. He wants to keep his options open until he sees which way the wind is blowing. We may be talking about an annulment or a deferment or a change in specs."

Lorraine smiled sweetly. "You mean, Sheridan Ireland may not decide what the views of Murren's selectmen are until halfway through the conference?"

"My God, what kind of way is that to talk? We're all on the same side, aren't we? It's just that Tristate has the—"

She interrupted him ruthlessly. "How much are they paying you?"

"Not a penny. Not what you could call payment, anyway." He began to lose himself in a welter of half-sentences. "Of course they'll take care of my expenses . . . well, you'd expect that, wouldn't you? And when a man has to leave a business that doesn't run itself, then he's so much out of pocket, and he's got a right to . . . but none of that means they're paying me. That's just business."

"We all knew you were picking up a little something on the side," she said, overriding his protests. "But there didn't seem that much harm in it at the beginning. Now, I'm not so sure."

Barry pulled out a handkerchief and wiped a suddenly feverish brow. "You've got no call to make it sound that way. Just because I'm getting a little compensation for helping people out in a good cause. You know I'm for Murren, all the way. For God's sake, you could say I'm going to Washington to keep an eye on Tristate."

"All right, George, you go keep an eye on Ireland." Then she grinned at him before adding, "But I'm going—to keep an eye on you!"

CHAPTER 19

Ben, meanwhile, was wrestling with a different problem altogether.

"No, I don't want to talk to Elsie about it," Tony Martinelli said truculently.

"But, Tony!" Ben tried to be reasonable. "You want to pressure the Defense Department and Elsie is on Armed Services. Why traipse all the way out to Virginia, when we can walk across the hall?"

"Because Elsie's never been in a tank, that's why!"

Ben had to concede that this was pretty unanswerable. Despite widely divergent political ideals, moral values and life styles, Elsie Hollenbach and Tony Martinelli were fast friends. They respected each other's opinion, they valued each other's savvy. Tony regularly crossed party lines to consult Elsie about the habits of the affluent suburbs. Elsie regarded Tony as Congress' authority on the decay of core city. But when it came to military policy, they parted company.

Naturally, they shared the legislator's ingrained contempt for those four-star wonders in the Pentagon. But there all similarity ceased. Elsie, who had never encountered the military until she was handling its purse strings, regarded the Joint Chiefs as so many backward students. Convinced that she knew more about long-term strategy than they did, she labored scrupulously to improve their minds.

Tony, on the other hand, had first tangled with the army during World War II. Inside a tank, he had invaded North Africa, been pinned down at Anzio, and crossed the Rhine. These experiences had left an indelible impression.

"Believe me, Ben, there's no such thing as military strategy. All there is, is a voice barking at you from the radio, ordering the unit to do things that are crazy. See, when the brass makes all those fancy plans, they forget the other guy is going to do something, too. So, they get thrown out of whack, right at the start. Then everybody rushes around, trying to plug the dike."

As far as Tony was concerned, the army was a machine for burning money. He was too much of a realist to think he could stop the habit. He only wanted to make them burn as much as possible in Rhode Island.

"Do you know what our unemployment rate is?" he would ask earnestly. "The country's got the biggest defense budget ever, and my district is losing jobs!"

"Yes, yes," said Ben hastily. He did not want a rerun of Tony's theory that the army always spends more money in peacetime because the Pentagon has nothing else to do.

"No, I'll lay it on the line to General Carson. And if you're there to back me up, Ben, he'll know that this retirement bill of his is in for a hard time unless he co-operates. But Elsie!" Tony flung his arms wide. "Try talking about the Pentagon with her, and you'll end up counting fueling stops in the Indian Ocean."

Ben grinned. "It isn't as bad as that, Tony, but I can see I'll save time in the end by going over with you." He paused. "And you'll remember this when the soybean price supports come up, won't you?"

"Ben," said Tony, with deep reproach, "have I ever welshed? You come to me, no matter what it is—soybeans, cotton, anything!"

"We don't grow an awful lot of cotton in Ohio, Tony," Ben said. "Don't you ever get curious about all the agriculture bills you vote on?"

"Listen, if I want to be curious, there's plenty in Providence to keep me busy."

"All right, all right. Just let me return a couple of these calls Madge has been nagging me about, then we can go."

Dutifully he worked his way through Madge's list. The Speaker was unusually long-winded.

"I've had the auto workers, the building trades people and the meat packers union on my neck, Ben," he bawled. "They all want to know what these lazy, good-for-nothing Democrats are doing about the economy."

Ben pointed out that General Motors, National Homes and Hormel were probably on the phone to Washington wanting to know what those lazy, good-for-nothing Republicans were doing.

"Crap!" said the Speaker.

As he grounded the receiver, Ben remarked, "You know, I think he's beginning to fray around the edges."

Before Tony could tell him all about the Speaker's latest bout with the Freshman Caucus, Madge appeared.

"It's Dean Kennison on the line," she reported. "I wouldn't bother you, but he insists that it's very important."

"That's all I need," grunted Ben, returning to the phone. "Good morning, Dean. This is Ben Safford."

"Good morning, Mr. Congressman," Kennison replied. "Sorry to break in on you like this without warning, but something has come up. I wonder, could I come over and see you right now? I'm at the Mayflower."

Involuntarily, Ben looked across the desk. Tony had already risen and was champing at the bit. Every minute of delay was obviously costing somebody in Providence a forty-hour-a-week job.

"You've caught me just as I was going out the door," Ben said. "What about this afternoon? I'll be free after—say, three o'clock."

"That will be too late," said Kennison heavily. He hesitated, organizing his argument. "I'd very much like to see you before I go up to the AEC after lunch. As you probably know, I've been doing some fairly intensive case studies of the power plants that are already in operation around the country."

"Yes, I know," said Ben grimly. "UBC has already hooked me for that panel of yours."

"I'm afraid I was responsible for that," Kennison replied awkwardly. "That's why I'm calling you. Before you say anything in public, you really should hear me out. Since I suggested your name to Proctor, there has been a development I never expected."

This measured and uninformative approach irritated Ben. The panel was still ten days off. He was not going to drop everything at a moment's notice.

"I'm sorry the timing isn't working out," Ben said. "I'm due at the Pentagon in fifteen minutes."

There was a sound of exasperation, then Ben could hear fingers drumming on a table. He waited. Kennison was the one who was all stirred up. Let him work out a solution.

Would he have the gall to suggest putting the Pentagon on hold?

But Kennison saw another way out. "If I'm right about my Washington geography, Mr. Congressman, you'll be passing directly in front of my hotel. Couldn't you stop off?"

"We-ll," Ben began doubtfully.

"It will only take a moment," said Kennison persuasively. "And I think you'll be glad of the warning—before the balloon goes up in Newburg."

Either this was reckless exaggeration or a real alert. Ben had to take his choice.

"I'll be there at noon," he said decisively.

In the taxicab, he explained the stopover to Tony.

"Kennison?" Tony savored the name. "Oh sure, he's the professor who was on TV."

"That's him," said Ben. "And he swore it wouldn't take more than a couple of minutes—whatever it is."

But Tony was not worrying about time. Single-minded as ever, he pursued his own concerns.

"That's what Providence needs," he announced. "A great big nuclear power plant."

"You're asking for trouble," said Ben from bitter experience. "Just thank God that they don't put them in the middle of big cities."

But he was addressing someone who had really listened to James Proctor and all his guests.

"Why not?" Tony demanded. "According to this professor of yours, if anything goes haywire, it poisons the water and the air for miles around. So, the cities are going to get it in the neck anyway. If they're going to get poisoned, they might as well get the jobs first."

"I don't think it's that simple," said Ben.

But the light of battle beamed from Tony's eyes. "Hell, half the time these bigwigs overlook the simple solution. Anyway, I can ask him."

"You do that," Ben urged him.

That should give Humphrey Kennison something to think about. A battle royal over building a reactor miles from anywhere, in Murren, balanced by an enthusiastic desire to plant one in the middle of Megalopolis.

The rest of their drive was enlivened by the growing complexity of Tony's scheme. Providence would become the power center of New England.

"No reason we couldn't supply Boston, and all Massachusetts," he said raptly. "They wouldn't want one up there. You know how they are."

Then the Defense Department couldn't miss the obvious advantage of new installations next to a limitless source of energy.

"Not just saving jobs, but creating new ones!"

By the time they pulled up at the Mayflower, Rhode Island had led the nation to independence from foreign oil.

"That's what they keep bugging us to do, isn't it?"

"You talk to Kennison about it," Ben repeated as he searched his pockets for a tip.

Fired by enthusiasm, Tony was well in the lead as they strode into the Mayflower lobby. But a quick survey failed to disclose the man he had watched on his twenty-one inch screen. Ben strolled over to the desk.

"Oh, yes, Congressman Safford," the receptionist said instantly. "Dr. Kennison called down about fifteen minutes ago. He asked that you go right up. It's room seven-eleven."

As they waited for the elevator, Ben was frowning.

"I expected him to be downstairs," he said slowly.

"What's the matter? You think he's trying to sucker you? Says he'll only take a minute, figuring that once you're up in his room he can drone away to his heart's content?"

Getting cornered is a well-known Washington hazard.

"No, that's not it," said Ben. "It's just that I'm beginning to wonder what he's got up his sleeve."

Tony put his intelligence to work. "It'll just take a minute," he said narrowly, "but he won't talk about it over the phone."

"And," said Ben, right there with him, "apparently he's afraid to talk about it in a hotel lobby."

In Tony's circles, the next question was inevitable. "Does he know you're bringing a witness, Ben?"

"I don't think so, but I'm beginning to be damned glad I've got one. You know, maybe I was too casual about all this. I just assumed that Kennison unearthed something technical. But he talked about a development he never expected. That could mean anything—including Davis Quentin."

Tony whistled softly as the elevator finally arrived. "You mean the guy who got bumped off in your district? You're sure you're not reaching, Ben?"

"I'm not sure of anything," said Ben, punching the button for the seventh floor. "But this smells a lot bigger than any TV panel."

"He wants something."

Ben shifted. "What have I got to give him?"

"He probably thinks you have pull with the feds. Most people back in my district think so. It's always a big disappointment to them when they get hauled in anyway."

Ben knew about the pained discoveries of some of Tony's friends. "But Kennison isn't like that," he said. "He's very knowledgeable about Washington and who pulls what strings."

"Sure, he's wise as long as he's playing in his own ball park. But let him move out a little, and he can get just as rattled as anybody else. If you're right, and he's found some real dirt—why, I bet he's plenty shook up."

Ben took a deep breath. "Well, here we are. Let's find out what the distinguished professor has to say."

In silence they marched down the corridor, following the arrow pointing to rooms 711–23.

Ben poised his knuckles. "Well, here goes!"

When a polite knock brought no response, Tony said, "He's busy."

"He should have taken care of that earlier," Ben grumbled, getting ready for a stronger assault.

This time his brisk rat-a-tat produced results. The lightly latched door swung inwards.

"I'll leave a note," said Ben, "but I'm not sitting around waiting for him."

But even as he stepped over the threshold, the words froze on his lips.

The crumpled body of Humphrey Kennison lay in front of the luggage rack. His fall had brought down the contents of his suitcase, strewing socks and underwear across the rug. But they did not hid the obscenity that had been Humphrey Kennison's head.

"My God," Tony whispered hoarsely, "they've blown his brains out!"

CHAPTER 20

After the first paralyzing shock, Ben backed out the door and raced for the nearest phone. He had barely returned to room 711 before uniformed men were pouring out the elevator. But it was with the arrival of the plainclothes men that the investigation really began. They were painstaking, methodical and deliberate. Several weary hours passed before the two congressmen were free to leave.

"Well, like Kennison said, the balloon went up, all right," Tony Martinelli philosophized.

"Yeah," said Ben. Right now, he did not want to think about Humphrey Kennison.

Neither did Martinelli. "Two more beers," he told the bartender.

Congressmen Martinelli and Safford were hiding out in a seedy tavern in SW while the first wave of reporters broke on their hapless offices. The best part of the afternoon was already gone. Not even Tony had enough strength left for General Carson and the Pentagon.

"I suppose we should get moving," Ben said unwillingly.

"Give it ten-fifteen minutes more, to be on the safe side," said Tony, consulting his watch. "That way we can at least duck the early TV news."

As usual, he was rolling with the punches.

Ben winced. "I'm sorry about a lot of things," he said somberly, "and one of them is that I dragged you into this. It's going to be a mess."

Tony did not deny it, but with a shrug, said, "That's life. And it could be worse. Finding a body is not so hot, I agree. But it beats falling into the Reflecting Pool, with a stripper."

Ben smiled reluctantly and the horror that had been Humphrey Kennison receded a step further.

"Besides," said Tony broodingly, "it's been a real education. I like to know how the boys are playing things."

Ben saw Kennison's murder in terms of Murren, and people he knew. Tony saw headlines.

"So," he had explained, "a few telephone calls can't hurt. Lou's on the District Committee. I'll get him to put in a good word for us. Tell the mayor to play this thing close to the chest. With luck, they'll catch the murderer and keep us out of the whole thing."

But those days were over, at least temporarily. Since Watergate, the District Police and the FBI were walking the straight and narrow with a vengeance. Far from suppressing names, they were garnering them. One look at Humphrey Kennison's notebook had been enough for Captain Gillis to send a man out to the AEC.

He returned with an air of suppressed excitement—and half the Washington press corps.

Tony got more out of the AP man than he gave. "Somebody tipped these guys off that all hell was going to break loose at the AEC," he told Ben. "They were already nosing around there, waiting for Kennison to light the match. When they heard he got knocked off, they came tearing back here."

Meanwhile, Captain Gillis had been listening to his subordinate's report.

"Congressman Safford," he said, strolling over, "what can you tell me about these people?" He consulted a list. "Sheridan Ireland . . . Lorraine Westerfeld . . . Roger Gladstone . . . George Barry . . . or Paul Carr?"

*   *

"Still, you two fellas may have been lucky after all," Val Oakes said the next morning before the subcommittee came to order.

Elsie Hollenbach sniffed eloquently.

"Well, it wasn't their fault this professor got himself killed," Val told her.

"I didn't even know the guy," said Tony virtuously.

"Ben," asked Mrs. Hollenbach, "have the police told you anything?"

"Nothing they haven't told the papers, too," said Ben forcefully. "Sorry, Elsie, I didn't mean to shout at you. But I was up half the night telling people that."

Janet had called. Ed Daly had called. And so had every television station in Ohio.

"The papers are not very informative," Elsie said accusingly.

"I know," said Ben. The hard facts were few and far between. Somebody had entered Humphrey Kennison's room at the Mayflower late Tuesday morning, and shot him. The time frame was pretty well established: between twelve o'clock, when he had phoned the desk, and twelve fifteen, when Ben and Tony arrived—in other words, less than two hours before Kennison was scheduled to explode his bombshell at the AEC.

As for who had pulled the trigger, the police were saying nothing. But there were plenty of suspects in Washington and too damned many of them came from Ohio's Fiftieth for Ben's peace of mind.

"Just thank your lucky stars that the Portuguese Army is such a bunch of duds," said Val.

"You know," Tony said radiantly, "there's a big Portuguese vote in Providence."

Unlike Ben, he could count his blessings. Tumult in Lisbon, with a raggletaggle alliance of unarmed civilians trouncing the troops, had overshadowed Humphrey Kennison in Rhode Island headlines.

"Just like that time Khrushchev died," said Tony. "It got that White House guy off the hook. You remember, the one who got into trouble in the YMCA?"

"The good Lord moves in mysterious ways," said Val sonorously. "And, in Washington, in mighty peculiar places."

Elsie had been following this exchange with disapproval. Ben had not been following it at all. Instead, he found himself thinking of another Oakes aphorism. Before things get better, they usually get worse.

*   *

Madge had proof waiting for him.

"You might as well sit down," she said when he halted by her desk. "The list of people who want you to call back would sink a ship."

"It's nice to be so popular," said Ben.

Madge simply started in. "Captain Gillis, of the District Police wants to talk to you. So does Agent Unsell—he's the FBI—"

"I know," said Ben. "Maybe I should say in demand."

Also eager to contact Congressman Safford were the Speaker, Mr. Andrew Heisse, Mr. Sheridan Ireland, the Democratic Whip and James Proctor.

"I suppose I should have foreseen that," said Ben once he digested the last name in the hopper. "Proctor made Kennison into a celebrity. He probably thinks he's got a vested interest in the murder."

Madge nibbled her pencil thoughtfully. "UBC reported the murder last night," she said. "And Proctor closed with a short tribute. What more do you suppose he can be planning?"

In twenty-four hours, they both found out.

". . . struck down in cold blood," said James Proctor starkly. "Who did it, and why? To date, the police don't really know. Our staff learns that hours of investigation, questioning everybody from Congressman Safford and the AEC to the president of Tristate and Lorraine Westerfeld—who joined Dr. Kennison on this program just a few weeks ago—has produced no solid leads. What we know is that Humphrey Kennison is dead. I shall miss him, as I know many of you will, too. And, in that spirit, we went this afternoon to talk to Dean Kennison's daughter. Mrs. Carr . . ."

When the camera panned onto Abby, Ben felt as though he had been hit in the solar plexus. The terrible TV fascination with victims, survivors and sufferers was always an abomination. The prospect of anybody he knew bleeding in public made him feel queasy.

"You can look now, Ben," said Elsie Hollenbach with the sympathy of the strong. "She seems to have herself in hand."

Ben forced himself to sit still.

Abby Carr had the heartbreaking solemnity of a child who has

wept until there are no more tears. Sometimes the right word
would not come.

". . . hope to continue as . . . as my father would have
wanted . . ."

"That's Lafayette Park, isn't it?" Madge commented as the
camera showed Abby brushing hair off her forehead. "Did they
call her up to Washington or was she here, when her father was
killed?"

"Lorraine Westerfeld tells me that Carr came up for the meeting alone," he said. "Abby didn't come until they broke the news
to her."

"So, Paul Carr was on his own," said Madge significantly.

This produced a receptive silence for James Proctor's next
comment.

"We have already learned of Humphrey Kennison's work to
improve the quality of life throughout the world. Lately, he had
been concentrating on nuclear safety here in the United States."

"That's right," Abby chimed in eagerly. "As soon as my father
returned from abroad, he joined our crusade to insure a pure environment, free from radioactive contamination."

Proctor wanted to talk about Dean Kennison, not PEP.

"Yes," he said warmly. "Your father applied his vast knowledge of hydrodynamics to the search for safe utilization of the
abundant natural resources that this nation possesses."

But since Kennison's death, Abby had convinced herself that
her father and her husband had been marching together in common cause.

"Oh, no," she said sincerely. "My father knew better than anyone the danger of having reactors close to communities where
people are raising their children."

Proctor recognized her rhetoric, but misjudged her tenacity of
purpose. He tried once again to get back on track. "Don't you
agree, Mrs. Carr, that it was his unique combination of technical
genius and balanced judgment in weighing conflicting interests
that made your father's death such a tragic loss to all of us?"

She squared her shoulders. Where James Proctor saw complexity, Abby saw simplicity.

"When it's a question of right or wrong, the decision may be
hard, but it's not complicated," she declared passionately.

"Daddy knew what they were trying to do to Newburg County. Tristate has used every trick they could to silence our protest. We've been thrown out of meetings. We've been libeled in the newspapers. And now, Daddy is dead!"

Ben, Elsie and Madge, like the rest of James Proctor's viewers, could not see the signal he must have made to his producer. But, as UBC's evening news closed, an unseen voice intoned a precautionary formula, "The opinions you have heard expressed on this program do not necessarily reflect the views of the network or . . ."

*   *

If ever an occasion called for equal time, this was it. Tristate's outraged demand was honored immediately.

Sheridan Ireland himself read the message into the microphone. Making no attempt to conceal his fury, he announced in a shaking voice, ". . . no irresponsible radical accusations are going to prevent Tristate Consolidated Electric from proceeding with its plans to serve the communities of southern Ohio to the best of its ability. Buckeye Atomic will be in operation right on schedule. The benefits we expect—"

Here Ireland choked, then angrily threw away the text.

"There's been a helluva lot of trouble," he rumbled, "but we haven't been making it. And, I give you my word, we don't intend to let it stop us!"

CHAPTER 21

United Broadcasting, with its proprietary interest in Dean Humphrey Kennison, had pulled out all stops in covering his murder. But the combination of two mysterious slayings, a disputed nuclear reactor and a Washington locale was too news-worthy for the other networks to overlook. And where television led, the papers and the magazines followed.

Soon all the interested parties were moving under a blaze of publicity. Lorraine Westerfeld was regularly using the service entrance at the Shoreham. Five floors above her, Sheridan Ireland had imported two PR men as buffers, but he was still glad to learn the backstairs geography from Mrs. Westerfeld. Poor Mrs. Davis Quentin's visit to her husband's grave was turned into a howling nightmare.

Nor were the police exempt from the spotlight. With every-body from the President to the National Academy of Science de-manding results, with the FBI and the Department of Justice muscling in, Captain Gillis was under fire from the moment he took charge. But at the end of three days his efforts had not pro-duced one single lead, and every investigator circling the death of Humphrey Kennison was reduced to asking the same people the same questions.

Ben Safford, for instance, was asked about three items over and over again. When he searched the Mayflower lobby for Dean Kennison, had he recognized anyone? When he entered the Up elevator, had he received any impression, however vague, of those emerging from the Down elevator? Could he remember anything at all about the condition of the corridor leading to room 711? Was there somebody whisking around a corner, was there a door swinging softly closed, was there a sound of footsteps on the metallic fire stairs? In spite of his blanket denials, the law enforcement agencies of Washington were convinced that, sooner or later, his memory would stir to life.

During his many terms as a congressman, Ben thought he had mastered the district's geography. But during the course of that week he learned all sorts of new corners. He became hardened not only to going to strange places to be interviewed, but to seeing familiar faces on the way.

When he began to trudge up the steps of police headquarters that Friday, he was not surprised to see Roger Gladstone trudging down.

"Hello, Gladstone. We haven't met since yesterday."

"At the FBI," Gladstone agreed with a weary nod.

Ben paused, willing to defer Captain Gillis for a few minutes. "Well, you can't deny that the police know how to put the pressure on."

"They're not the only ones!"

The underlining was so clear that Ben raised an eyebrow. "I guess I've missed something."

"Haven't you heard, Congressman?" Gladstone chose his words with care. "The AEC and Lomax Tool have agreed on a slight delay in the Buckeye construction permit. Not for publication, of course."

The last was so obvious that Ben ignored it. "That's funny," he said. "I could have sworn I heard Sheridan Ireland telling the world that Buckeye was going ahead on target."

"Sheridan Ireland can scream his head off, for all I care!" Gladstone colored. "Sorry, but I'm fed up with Ireland making a monkey of himself."

Ben was thoughtful. "I don't know about that. Abby Carr practically accused him of murder. I would have been plenty mad, myself."

"I'm not talking about that. Although, if you ask me, he over-reacted. He would have been better off ignoring her. But the real problem isn't Abby Carr. It's the fact that Humphrey Kennison was murdered. We've got two bodies hanging around Buckeye's

neck like an albatross. And all Ireland can say is damn the tor-
pedos, full speed ahead."

Ben could sympathize with anyone at close quarters to Sheridan Ireland. "And you don't like to operate that way?"

"I can't afford to," Gladstone said frankly. "Ireland is in the
utility business. Buckeye will probably be his one and only
atomic installation."

"Whereas Lomax Tool . . ."

"Lomax Tool is in the nuclear business. The AEC is our bread
and butter. And when your bread and butter wants a little co-
operation, you deliver."

Ben did his calculating aloud. "The AEC is clutched up about
these two murders. They don't want to go forward until they
know what gives. But they don't want to back down publicly.
Meanwhile, Ireland makes things worse by clamoring for speed.
So . . ." his voice trailed away.

"So," Gladstone concluded with a humorless smile, "Lomax
Tool discovers it wants to make some design modifications that
will take a couple of months, and the AEC gives a great big sigh
of relief at getting off the hook."

Deals of this sort are being made on Constitution Avenue
every hour.

"And they say that the AEC is a pawn in your pocket!"

Gladstone had spotted a cruising cab and raised a hand to hail
it. "They should try tangling with that kind of pawn," he
snorted as he loped down to the curb. "They'd end up mince-
meat."

Ben grinned as he continued into headquarters. He did not
swallow this story for one minute. But he could understand the
AEC engaging in some uncharacteristic arm twisting. This was a
good time to shake the pawn-of-industry image.

He arrived at the captain's office before he could pursue these
thoughts. Instead of being alone, Gillis was entertaining a hefty
young man in civilian clothes.

"They told me to come right in, Captain, but I can come back
another day if you're busy," Ben said hopefully.

The stranger looked up. "I bet you don't recognize me out of
uniform, Congressman."

The touch of downstate Ohio was just strong enough to rescue Ben.

"Why, it's Lieutenant Youngman," he began. Then Janet's mantle descended on him. "Let's see, you're Carolyn Orford's brother, aren't you? I hear she's back from the Coast."

Captain Gillis let them bring each other up-to-date on the Orford family before calling the meeting to order.

"The State Police in Ohio thought we better have some liaison on these two murders, Congressman," he explained, "and they sent along the lieutenant. We're damned glad to have him. This investigation needs more police and fewer bureaucrats."

"Don't get your hopes up," advised Tommy Youngman. "That killing in Murren was too close to a perfect murder. There was so much milling around that everyone had the opportunity. The weapon was a rock lying on the ground. And as far as motive goes, we still don't know whether Quentin was killed because he was going to nix the whole Buckeye project or because he was giving it a go-ahead. No, I figure you're going to be a lot more help to me, than I am to you."

Captain Gillis agreed gloomily. "It's pretty much the same can of worms with us. We can't prove anything about the weapon. According to ballistics, it was used in a robbery in Chicago seven years ago. It's probably changed hands twenty times since then. And everybody involved with Kennison was chasing around Washington without an alibi." For a moment, white teeth glinted against tanned skin. "Except the Congressman, here."

Ben reflected that Tony Martinelli's value as a witness was proving greater than expected. He decided to see how far the Captain was ready to admit him into his confidence. "Everybody?" he asked. "It doesn't seem natural that not one single person has an alibi."

"You've got to remember that this was lunch hour." Gillis took his time, weighing the merits of calculated indiscretion. Then he continued, very deliberately. "Take Mr. Heisse, for example. It only takes him fifteen minutes to get home, so he has lunch there once or twice a week. That's where he was, and he was alone because his wife was off with some women's group. And that fits in with Mr. Vorhees' story. He lunches with the Commissioner frequently, but not regularly. Around quarter to twelve, he looked into Heisse's office. When he couldn't find him, he went off to eat on his own. And that Roger Gladstone. He doesn't make any secret of the fact that he was hopping with curiosity about Kennison's conference. He got into town the night before, shot over to the AEC first thing in the morning, pumped the archives people about what Kennison was reading, got copies for himself and went back to the Statler. He ordered up a stack of sandwiches at eleven-thirty and settled down to read every word he could, before the two o'clock deadline. So you see, they've all got reasonable explanations for being alone."

Ben appreciated the delicacy with which the captain had told him that the Washington police weren't taking anyone on faith.

"And the others are the same?"

"Insofar as they don't have alibis. But a couple of peculiar things cropped up. And mostly they concern people from your bailiwick."

Gillis was enjoying himself, Tommy Youngman was sitting up expectantly, and Ben Safford was braced for the worst.

"Take that George Barry and Mrs. Westerfeld. They flew in together during the morning, but as soon as they landed Barry cut off by himself, telling Mrs. Westerfeld he'd see her over at the AEC at two o'clock. So she was on her own from ten-thirty on. She checked into her hotel, then went to Garfinkel's to return some things, then grabbed a bite—"

He was interrupted by a braying laugh from Lieutenant Youngman. "If you're seriously trying to work up a case against Lorraine, maybe I'd better retire," he said with a broad grin. "She and my mother are some kind of cousins, and I used to date her daughter. If you're that hard up, this murder is hopeless."

"No, it's not her I'm talking about, it's him. Because Barry's story was that he just wandered around for three hours, seeing the sights. He made the mistake of mentioning a few of them, and it was a cinch to catch him out. The man's never been on top of the Washington Monument in his life."

Tommy Youngman liked the sound of this better. "What did Barry say then?"

"He didn't. He clammed up and said he knew his rights. I got at it another way." For the first time Captain Gillis smiled. "I remembered that Sheridan Ireland's alibi had bothered me. According to him, he was sitting in his room at the Shoreham, alone, from ten-thirty until he took a cab to the AEC. He never went to the restaurant, never called room service. So I gave him a second go-round, and I leaned on him a little."

"And I suppose he remembered his rights, too?" Tommy asked sourly.

"No. He may be used to acting like a tin-pot god, but he's got some sense. He's not courting suspicion of a double murder just to cover up something petty. He finally admitted that George Barry is on his payroll."

Without realizing it, Safford and Tommy Youngman were nodding appreciatively.

"That explains a lot," said Ben. "Were they having a secret meeting?"

"That's the funny part. Barry was supposed to go straight to Ireland's room from the airport. But he didn't show up until one o'clock. Once Ireland spilled the beans, Barry explained that he forgot to find out Ireland's hotel. He says he spent the time going from one registration desk to another."

Tommy considered this. "It could be."

"Oh, he went to some. We've checked. But his schedule is full of holes. So the upshot is that either one of them could have dropped in on Kennison at noon."

Ben had been doing some internal arithmetic and had spotted the omission. "Is that what you meant by people from my baili-wick? Barry and Lorraine?"

"Not exactly. I've been saving the best for last." Gillis tilted his head and examined the ceiling with a wooden expression. "Paul Carr, the Dean's son-in-law, spent the morning in Nina Yeager's apartment—"

"Wait a minute!" Lieutenant Youngman was holding up a traffic cop's hand. "Who's she? The girl friend?"

"Apparently not. Instead, she's the leak at the AEC who's been feeding him material. The FBI's known about it for weeks. She and Carr were playing the same game as Gladstone, trying to find out what Kennison had up his sleeve. She pulled a lot of stuff from the office files for Carr to read."

"Has the FBI told Heisse about this?" Ben asked curiously.

"Not on your life." Gillis laughed shortly. "He told the FBI he was going to run his own operation, and they're taking him at his word. But what the hell! I don't care what little ploys they work on each other, so long as they don't interfere with my case. And the important thing is that Carr left Yeager's place at eleven-thirty, went back to his hotel to wash up, and was in the coffee shop at twelve-fifteen ordering his lunch."

"But you said . . ." Youngman blinked furiously, looking for the catch. "Then Carr has an alibi, doesn't he?"

"Except for one little thing. Although he claims he didn't know where his father-in-law was staying, Paul Carr checked into the Mayflower—into room 611."

"Great!" For a moment Youngman was discouraged into silence. Then he changed course. "All right, I grant you that opportunity isn't getting us anywhere. But what about motive? If Kennison called all these people to an emergency meeting about Buckeye, then he was going to blow it up. There wouldn't be a crisis if he was going to okay it. So that narrows things, doesn't it?"

But Captain Gillis was shaking his head. "I'm not so sure. That's what I wanted to talk to the Congressman about."

Ben had been wondering about his role in this informal conference. "I'll be glad to help if I can," he said warily.

"According to the story we've got, Kennison hit something so big that a commissioner at the AEC has to drop everything, and a congressman has to detour on his way to the Pentagon, to hear him out. Well, Mr. Safford, you know a little about this guy Kennison. Under these circumstances, would he have asked all these other people to sit in?"

Ben was beginning to see why Gillis wanted the opinion of an old Washington hand. "Not for a minute," he replied. "Kennison was treating this as confidential. The last thing he wanted was a mass meeting."

"That's what I thought. Either he was up to something—or his murderer was."

"How?" Ben asked.

"I'm not so sure Kennison made all these calls. The murderer may simply have added himself to the list to have a reason for coming to Washington."

Youngman was right with him. "Or the murderer could have made some of those calls."

"Absolutely. Carr was called at lunch time when he was out, Ireland was called in Cincinnati when he was in Washington. The only call I'll take as proven is the one to the AEC. The girl on the switchboard has heard Kennison's voice a lot and she'll swear it was him. Could you do as much, Congressman?"

Ben was momentarily taken aback. "No, I couldn't," he conceded at last. "I've only met Kennison once. I could easily have been fooled."

"What about Gladstone?" Youngman asked. "Kennison told the AEC he invited him."

"So Vorhees says," Gillis shot back. "But we don't know it. As far as I'm concerned, all the calls are suspect."

To make matters worse, there was no possibility of checking back from the victim's end.

"Kennison was bouncing around like a Ping-pong ball, from one reactor to another," the captain reported discontentedly. "His secretary got calls from Indiana and Illinois, from Michigan and Kentucky. She says half the time he used pay booths and direct dialed. And he didn't use a credit card, he got out of the habit overseas."

In the end they agreed that, in addition to contacting the AEC, Humphrey Kennison might have spoken to only one other person.

"But the wrong one," said Gillis grimly.

Both policemen seemed pleased at having established a clear field. Ben decided to leave on this note of accomplishment, pausing only to invite Tommy Youngman to dinner.

"I'm picking Lorraine up at six. Why don't you come along and we can have a quiet evening, forgetting about these murders," he said in one of the worst forecasts of his life.

*   *

Over at the AEC there was no pretense of forgetting the murders. In fact, they were being shoved down Sheridan Ireland's throat.

"Look, we're not on television now," rasped Andy Heisse, sounding a good deal tougher than he did in public. "Let's face facts. So far, we've got two bodies littering up this project. In my book, that means something stinks."

"You're supposed to be running this country's nuclear program." Ireland's jaw was rigid. "And you're going to let a bunch of longhairs throwing rocks stop the whole thing?"

"Kennison was no longhair. I don't say I liked his style, but—"

"Kennison was that woman's father!" Ireland interrupted.

"To hell with whose father he was. He pulled all the plans for Murren, he went on a tour of our midwestern installations, he talked to every expert we've got. Then he was excited enough to call a top-level conference, and boom! His brains are blown out!" Heisse choked and forced himself to stop shouting. "If you don't believe me, ask Roger here. He was in Indianapolis just after Kennison. I'll bet they told him Kennison was doing a damn thorough job."

Roger Gladstone looked annoyed at being sucked into the controversy, but he did his best. "That's right, Sherry," he said in a subdued tone. "I've told you from the beginning that Humphrey Kennison was a first-rate authority. You can't dismiss him."

"I'm not talking about Kennison," Ireland exploded. "I'm talking about this delay on Buckeye that you two are trying to pull. Don't you realize that I personally went on national television and pledged that we'd stick to the schedule?"

Heisse was at the end of his patience. "I don't give a damn what you pledged. If it comes to that, Paul Carr has pledged to stop Buckeye. Who do you all think you are? It's time you recognized that the AEC is making the rules in this ball park. And I'm not being blackmailed by any of you."

"Blackmail!" sputtered Ireland. "You're a fine one to talk. When, for no good reason—"

"What do you call a couple of killings? If that's not a reason—"

"You didn't call things off then. You waited until that woman went on Proctor's show."

"For Christ's sake, what does that have to do with anything?"

By now the two antagonists were both on their feet, glowering at each other across the polished expanse of Heisse's desk.

"Look, maybe we should all calm down." Reluctantly Gladstone intervened. "I'm sorry you're so upset about this deferment, Sherry, but after all it's only a matter of a couple of months."

"The delay has nothing to do with it, and you know it!" Ireland shot back without taking his eyes off Heisse. "How do you think this looks in the papers? The AEC stands firm on Buckeye until Mrs. Carr publicly brands me a murderer. Then they back off from the whole project as if I've got the plague. Do you think people can't read between the lines? You might just as well have gone on the six o'clock news and endorsed her."

"Why don't you try seeing somebody else's position for a change?" Heisse said heavily. He had sunk back into his chair and swiveled to include Gladstone in his remarks. "After Quentin's death, I agreed with you about not letting longhairs call the tune. But Kennison's murder changed all that. I don't know how, but in some way Buckeye is a ticking bomb. And I don't want to be around when it goes off. Then Gladstone comes in here and suggests some design modifications. Talk about people reading between the lines! How would it look if I refused to let a designer improve his specs just so I could ram Buckeye through, regardless of the consequences?"

It was a powerful appeal but it had no chance against Ireland's single-minded egotism.

"And in the meantime, what about me? The police are trying to build a case against me. They've been at my office in Cincinnati, they've been after my staff, and now I've been called down to headquarters. Like a common criminal!"

"You're overrefining," Heisse said curtly. "We've all been questioned."

"Maybe you're used to it!"

"What the hell is that supposed to mean?"

"You weren't so calm when the FBI wanted to see your files." Ireland's eyes were gleaming with malice. "Quentin and Kennison were both killed after they'd been nosing around a bunch of your installations. What kind of dirt were they likely to pick up?"

"Now just a minute!" Heisse had come bolt upright, slapping a meaty palm down on his desk.

"I'm not waiting any longer." Ireland was talking at such a furious pace that he began to stutter as his words tumbled over each other. "I recognize a put-up job when I see one. You and Gladstone are in this together, and you're trying to make me your patsy. You don't fool me with this crap about sudden design changes."

He had stormed his way to the door, paying no attention to the protests of the other two. But on the threshold he paused, the knob in his hand, for one final thrust.

"Well, you're not getting away with it!" he roared, slamming the door behind him like a pistol shot.

In the silence following his departure, Heisse and Gladstone stared blankly at each other. Then the commissioner unfurled a handkerchief and mopped his brow.

"That damned egomaniac. He's capable of anything when he's crossed," he muttered. "It's not as if there really is something for him to be desperate about."

Gladstone was so deep in thought he might not have heard.

"Well, there isn't, is there?" Heisse pleaded.

Gladstone's reply was a fraction too late. "Of course not," he said with a heartiness so false it echoed off the walls. "Not a thing in the world!"

CHAPTER 22

Sheridan Ireland was in a dangerous mood. The rage that had maddened him in Heisse's office had turned to ice by the time he reached Headquarters. But it remained, clamping him as tightly as a vise. When he left Captain Gillis, pain was throbbing at his temples and his breath was shallow and irregular.

The first double scotch helped; the scotches after that only fueled the flames. Ireland did not stagger as he crossed the Shoreham lobby to ask for messages, but he was at that emotional flashpoint where he saw solutions hidden from everybody else.

Swinging around, he collided with the woman behind him.

"I beg your pardon! Why, it's Mrs. . . . Mrs. . . . ."

"Westerfeld," said Lorraine.

"Just the person I want," said Ireland, seizing her arm. "Come over here with me."

He dragged her toward the nearest set of chairs without regard for her comfort. And he did not care who heard him, either. "You listen to me while I tell you what that SOB Gladstone is trying to pull!"

Lorraine rubbed the tender spot above her elbow while he pulled two chairs closer together. Instinct and experience told her that he needed careful handling.

"What about Gladstone?" she asked cautiously.

His suspicion spurted toward her. "You're not on his side, are you? You're not in favor of delaying Buckeye—"

"Why don't you just lower your voice and sit down," Lorraine snapped. She waited until he complied. "That's better. Now, I've already explained my position to George Barry, and

I'll explain it to you. Anybody with an ounce of sense or common decency has to see why some people think Buckeye should be held up for the time being"—there was a sudden catch in her throat which she ignored—"but I've decided the all-round best thing to do, for everybody concerned, is to go on."

Although Ireland listened intently, he heard only what he wanted to hear.

"There! That proves I'm right," he crowed. "If it was just Kennison's murder, someone like you'd be all for this delay, wouldn't you? But you think we should go on. So who's sniveling and backtracking? Not anybody who's really on our side. Just Mr. Roger Gladstone, who doesn't give a damn about anything but Number One!"

Lorraine was mystified by this outburst. Long ago, she had grasped Sheridan Ireland's methods and motives. His rank insensitivity to Humphrey Kennison's murder came as no revelation, and neither did his fixation on his own goals. But Ireland's tirade against Gladstone was as unexpected as his rough hands had been.

Maybe it was the drink.

Slowly and reasonably, she asked, "Don't you think there's room for an honest difference of opinion?"

Her humoring only turned him ugly. "You don't know what you're talking about!" But an insult was not enough. "Jesus Christ, an honest difference of opinion, the woman says! Hell, it's more like an honest stab in the back." The phrase pleased him, so he repeated it. "A stab in the back. Well, he's not getting away with it."

Scowling, he planted his hands on his knees long enough to make Lorraine hope that he might be losing steam. Then, without looking up, he began a bitter monotone, "It's a great little act, all right. Says his piece at the AEC, just the way he wants. Oh, it's great, great. To hell with Sherry Ireland and Tristate! No siree, Mr. Gladstone is going through the motions. It's important to double check the specs, it sure is. Why, that's what Mr. Gladstone's going to start doing right away, the minute he gets back to the Statler . . ."

He was talking to himself, but his dull persistence worried Lorraine.

"I don't understand a thing you're saying," she told him, half-angry, half-anxious.

With one of those treacherous quirks of the half-drunk, Ireland suddenly grew completely sober. "I don't see why not, Mrs. Westerfeld," he responded conversationally. "Surely you're one of the best people to comprehend the real arrogance behind this filthy scheme." He smiled benignly on her as if they were back in Murren. "After all, you're not a high-powered scientific expert, any more than I am. Well, let me tell you, these high-powered scientific experts think they're a lot smarter than the rest of the world. They think they're smarter than you are, Mrs. Westerfeld. And"—here, the old Ireland joviality dropped away like a discarded mask—"and smarter than Sheridan Ireland."

Lorraine knew all about the surface logic that liquor can produce and the dark confusions it can overlay. But she was shaken enough to try arguing, "It isn't just high-powered scientific experts who want to delay Buckeye—"

He did not let her finish. "They all go to the same places, don't they? They see the same things, don't they? What makes anybody think it takes an Einstein to add it all up? And come out with the right answer? You know, I've been in this business a long, long time! I've seen a thing or two—although never anything like this, I'll admit."

Utterly bewildered, she stared at him.

Her incomprehension infuriated him. "What's so hard to understand? Why are you gaping at me like that? I'm telling you the truth about Davis Quentin and Humphrey Kennison and Roger Gladstone, that's what I'm doing. Delay Buckeye—don't make me laugh!"

His parody of amusement was not pleasant to hear.

". . . that's how much I'll laugh . . . and I'll be the one who laughs last, that's for sure . . . he who lasts laugh . . . laughs last . . ."

"Mr. Ireland," she said as he slid further into incoherence. "Don't you think you should—"

"Well, this time it won't work. I'm blowing the whistle, right now." He leaped to his feet, swaying slightly. "I'm going right over there to teach Mr. Roger Gladstone a lesson about Sherry Ireland."

To her relief, he abruptly stopped shouting. Bending over, he hissed in her ear. "I'll let you in on a little secret. I'm going over to the Statler and I'm going to wring Mr. Roger Gladstone's neck!"

She recoiled before the blast of whiskey. "What you should do," she cried, "is go upstairs and sleep it off."

For a moment he loomed over her, breathing hard. Then, with a clumsy spin that nearly cost him his balance, he plunged toward the exit.

Lorraine sat tight and counted to ten. The more she thought about it, the more she was convinced that she had heard Sheridan Ireland, not liquor, talking.

"Sorry, ma'am." A young Marine, grazing her knees as he rushed past, woke her. The bustling Shoreham lobby had returned to normal after Ireland's conspicious exit. Couples meeting, tourists checking in, cigar-smoking husbands patiently waiting. In ten minutes, Ben Safford and Tommy Youngman would come through the doors, ready to take her to dinner. The sensible thing was to forget all about Sheridan Ireland.

"Like hell I will," said Lorraine, oblivious to the covert glances she was drawing. She looked around purposively. There were pay phones at the far wall. Half the trouble in the world, she thought, fumbling hurriedly for change, comes from people who are afraid to make fools of themselves.

"Mr. Roger Gladstone," she told the Statler firmly. If he wasn't in his room . . .

But a voice did answer. "Hello?"

"Mr. Gladstone, this is Lorraine Westerfeld," she announced. The hollow realization overcame her that marching to the phone was not going to be enough. "Er . . . I guess you're going to think this is a little strange . . ."

"Yes, Mrs. Westerfeld?" Gladstone was at least receptive.

Gulping, Lorraine forced herself on. She knew she could not convey Ireland's mood, so she relied on the bare bones of their encounter.

Gladstone did not scoff at her matter-of-fact recital.

"Oh, God!" he said tightly. "I've been afraid of something like this. It sounds as if Sherry's really gone round the bend. You know, he's been under a lot of strain and somehow or other

Abby Carr's performance on TV was the last straw. He was pretty wild this afternoon, over at the AEC. A couple of the things he was saying didn't make sense."

"It wasn't Abby Carr he was making threats about," said Lorraine bluntly, "it was you."

Gladstone's laugh was constrained. "You should have heard him going after Andy Heisse. Sherry doesn't like opposition, especially from somebody he thinks is on his team—"

"Look, Mr. Gladstone, he wasn't joking," said Lorraine with desperate exasperation. "I didn't call up to make polite conversation, either. I'm telling you that Ireland is in a real mean mood, and he was talking about murdering you—not a lot of other people. If you want my opinion, that's something to take seriously."

There was a long silence that rattled Lorraine. Did Gladstone think she was hysterical? Doubt began to chip away at her resolve.

"Of course, maybe I'm making too much of it," she said reluctantly. "What with Humphrey, and Davis Quentin and all! God knows, the man's got a right to have a few drinks—"

"To be honest with you," Gladstone broke in, "that bothers me more than anything else you've said. Sherry's no soak. But he's got a pretty hard head. I've seen him put away the best part of a bottle—and not show a thing. When you say he was drunk—well, it doesn't ring true to me."

Just as the implications of this remark sank in, the operator intervened. Numbly, Lorraine fed nickles and dimes into the slot. Could Sheridan Ireland have been faking?

"Oh, my God," she gasped, but Gladstone was already talking.

". . . try to reason with him, or talk sense to him—if he gives me the chance. Otherwise—"

"I think you should call the police," Lorraine blurted.

Again, there was a protracted silence.

"No," said Gladstone finally. "No, that wouldn't be fair. Look, Mrs. Westerfeld, Sherry's a troubled man. If we get the police involved, well, God knows where it will end. No"—he seemed to be convincing himself—"no, I can handle him on my own. That's the best way. But thanks for alerting me. Now, I can take some precautions."

"Wait a minute," she burst out. "You didn't hear how he

sounded. This could be dangerous. What if Ireland has a gun? Mr. Gladstone? . . . Mr. Gladstone?"

But the line was dead. And there was an impatient young man, waiting. Lorraine got out of his way, then halted. She was hovering in painful indecision when Ben Safford and Tommy Youngman caught sight of her.

"Hi, Lorraine!" Tommy began cheerfully.

"Thank God you're here." Lorraine was still shaken. "Maybe I'm going crazy, but I'm afraid there's going to be another murder."

Lieutenant Youngman went back on duty fast. "Hold it," he ordered. "Why don't you start from the top?"

Lorraine took a deep breath and tried to recreate her astonishing passage with Sheridan Ireland.

"You're sure it wasn't just because he was drunk?" Ben asked when she had finished.

"I'm not sure of anything," she wailed. "Obviously he had had a couple. But when I told Gladstone that, he told me Ireland can handle his liquor."

"It hits people harder when they're under pressure," Tommy said clinically.

"Oh, sure," Lorraine said. "Plenty of people talk big when they've had one too many. But Ireland was different, somehow. If he'd just gone on about Humphrey and Davis Quentin and Gladstone all ganging together, I wouldn't have paid any attention."

Ben opened his mouth to comment, but Lorraine had more unburdening to do. "But when it came to threats and the way he made them—well, to be honest, he scared me."

Tommy stuck to the point. "Did it scare Gladstone?"

"Not at first," she said slowly. Then in a rush, she added, "But when I told him that Ireland was making a dead set for him, Gladstone did say he'd take some precautious. I don't know why he won't call the police. Because I can tell he thinks Ireland is out of his mind."

Tommy Youngman muttered something about jurisdictions, while Ben remained lost in his own calculations.

"But that can't be right," Lorraine said, seeking reassurance.

"People like Sheridan Ireland don't turn into homicidal maniacs overnight, do they?"

All Ben had needed was a starting point. "But what if he isn't a homicidal maniac?" he asked slowly. "What if Ireland told you the plain, unvarnished truth, Lorraine?" As he spoke he saw a tangled mass of contradictions dissolve into an ominously simple pattern. "Because I think that may be what he did do—tell the truth. In which case, we'd better move pretty damn fast."

Appalled, Lorraine could only stare.

"Come on!" Ben barked, steering Tommy ahead of him.

"But Ben—"

"What do you want—"

"Good God, are you still standing there, Lorraine!" he yelled over his shoulder. "How much time do you think there is? Get moving! Call Gillis and put some muscle into it. Tommy and I will try to get to the Statler in time—if it's not too late already!"

*   *

Even without sirens, Safford and Tommy Youngman got to the Statler minutes before Captain Gillis and the Washington police. The margin was too slim for comfort.

"Come on," Ben huffed, breaking into a run toward the elevator. "Or, no! The stairs will be faster—"

Youngman galloped ahead of him. "But what—"

"Don't stop to argue," Ben yelled. "Move! MOVE!"

The fourth floor was already convulsed when Tommy and Ben burst through.

". . . sounds as if those guys in 423 are killing each other . . ."

"Has anybody called the desk?"

"Desk, hell, somebody call the cops!"

The hotel guests dithering in the hall scattered before Tommy's pounding drive. Ben, a poor second, was almost stopped cold when they regrouped in his path. But he thrust them aside to reach Tommy just as a kick crashed the door open.

Then he braked.

Roger Gladstone and Sheridan Ireland were in the center of the room, locked in a grotesque embrace. Gladstone's face was contorted with agonized effort as he inched the older man back. Ireland hunched forward, jamming his shoulder into his antagonist's chest, while a muscular arm arched Gladstone's back to the breaking point.

"Ae-ee-ee-ee!" With an Indian yell, Tommy Youngman jumped them, jolting them apart with his flying two hundred and fifteen pounds.

Ireland sank to his knees, semi-conscious. Then, with a groan, he fell face forward onto the bed, cradling his head in his arms as if warding off a blow.

Gladstone dazedly tried to speak. "I . . . he rushed me . . . didn't expect . . ."

White-faced and drained, he sagged against the bureau.

Tommy stood between them like a young Colossus. Without moving his head, he addressed Ben who was still frozen in the doorway. "You were right, Mr. Safford. We didn't have a lot of time to spare. But we managed it—and I guess we've got ourselves the murderer."

Ben was dimly conscious of noises behind him. There was excited twittering from the guests, and farther off, official sounds, deeper, more masculine. Once he caught his breath, he was going to have a lot of explaining to do.

About a change of schedule, a change of heart and, most important of all, a change of cast.

But just now, with the Washington police on their heels, the honor of Ohio was at stake. Wheezing heavily, Ben cued Tommy on the next speech.

"We've got ourselves the murderer, all right. But he's the one with the gun, Tommy. Him—Roger Gladstone!"

CHAPTER 23

"So it really was Roger Gladstone all the time!" Lorraine Westerfeld marveled. "I was sure you were making some kind of terrible mistake."

Ben was pleased to hear her sound relaxed and comfortable. He had organized this farewell dinner as a tribute to Lorraine's share in solving the Buckeye murders and as compensation for the evening shattered by his mad dash to the Statler. But after seating his guests at the table for five, he had suffered last-minute qualms. Val could be relied on to charm any lady in the land. And Tony would provide Lorraine with an exciting glimpse into another world. But Elsie? There was no denying that Mrs. Hollenbach's reaction to, and affect on, other women was incalculable.

During the first round of drinks the issue had trembled in the balance. Elsie had been at her most pontifical. Mrs. Westerfeld had retreated into white-gloved gentility. Then a lucky remark about oil prices had saved the day. Lorraine forgot herself long enough to chatter about the filling station. Mrs. Hollenbach unbent sufficiently to ask about catalytic converters. The men all held their breath and finally, in a miracle of tact, Elsie made a rare reference to the late Congressman Henry Hollenbach. Lorraine immediately shed the last vestige of restraint. She didn't pretend to understand women who ran for Congress on their own, but she knew all about widows taking over their husbands' business.

Now, with cordiality reigning, everyone felt free to talk about what was really interesting.

"By that time, Ireland and Gladstone had confused things

enough so that a lot of mistakes were possible," Ben agreed, signaling the waiter for another bottle of wine. When a party looked this promising, he believed in fueling it along.

"Then how did you know?" Lorraine pressed. "It was Mr. Ireland who was threatening blue murder. And he looked capable of anything when he rushed off and left me."

"I'll bet he did. He had just figured out what Gladstone was up to, and he's not the man to exercise much control."

Elsie coughed. But it was a far cry from her famous committee cough. This one was more punctuation than reproach. "Perhaps it would be better," she said, peering benevolently over her glass at the gathering, "if we started at the beginning."

"That's easy enough. And I can give you the whole progression while I'm at it," said Ben. "The beginning was when Roger Gladstone murdered Inspector Quentin. The middle was when he murdered Kennison. And the end was when Tommy Youngman arrested him in the act of trying to kill Sheridan Ireland."

Until now Val Oakes had been lost in the pleasures of the table, but he roused himself to pass judgment on two matters.

"That sounds nice and tidy, Ben, but I do believe you've left a few things out, such as the Murren referendum and the Carrs and that libel suit. They could stand a tolerable amount of explaining." He paused before going on to the weightier item. "And this wine isn't half bad. Ordinarily I don't hold with fancy brews, but there's no denying this one slides down smooth and promotes good conversation." Incorrigibly gallant, he toasted the ladies before settling back to hear Ben out.

There was general relief at his approval. It was always risky offering Val anything less than eighty-six proof.

Reassured, Ben proceeded. "I deliberately stripped the situation down to its basic elements because our confusion, all along, has been due to the trimmings. Take away PEP marching around the Murren Grange and George Barry lining his pockets and Nina Yeager slipping memos to Paul Carr, and what do you have?"

Tony Martinelli was more at home with this kind of residue than anybody else at the table. "You've got two bodies," he said promptly. "Both with their brains all over the place."

"They had more in common than that. Each of the victims had been examining a series of nuclear power installations."

"But, Ben," Lorraine protested, "that might mean something in Humphrey's case, because it wasn't the sort of thing he was used to doing. But it was Inspector Quentin's job! Any time he was killed he was likely to be making one of his routine trips."

"Except that it had stopped being routine," Ben pointed out. "The other common element was that both men broke their schedules in order to hightail it back to Washington. Long before they were expected at the AEC, they discovered something that made it essential to consult with headquarters."

Elsie Hollenbach sounded like a kindly fourth-grade teacher encouraging a pupil. "I seem to recall that factor received consideration after Inspector Quentin's death. The FBI thought it might have a possible bearing on his murder."

"With Davis Quentin dead, it was possible. With Humphrey Kennison dead in the same circumstances, it became a certainty. And that told us a lot about the murderer."

Lorraine Westerfeld was in top form. Gone was any shyness about dining with a big slice of Congress. Gone was any deference to the wisdom and experience of her representative. Gone was any worry about what the head waiter would think.

"What, for instance?" she challenged.

Ben was ready for her. "With Quentin and Kennison killed to stop them blabbing to the AEC, the murderer had to be somebody whose whole future was committed to the atomic energy program. That eliminated all the people who just had a temporary connection with the program. More specifically, all the people who were interested in Buckeye alone. They simply didn't have enough riding on it to explain two murders. Take Paul Carr. He was an ambitious young man trying to milk the situation in Murren for all it was worth. It's barely conceivable that he might have worked himself into a rage with Davis Quentin and picked up a rock before he knew what he was doing. But there was no systematic involvement with reactors that could have made Kennison find out something in Illinois or Kentucky that endangered Carr."

"I see that." Lorraine's brow was wrinkled thoughtfully. "And the same thing holds for George Barry. Even if he's been silly enough to pick up some real estate in Murren and wants to protect his investment, it isn't the sort of thing that Humphrey would have learned on his trips. But what about Sheridan Ireland? He's not a local, and his company has sunk a lot of money into nuclear power. Besides, he goes wild when he's crossed."

"He may not be a local from your point of view, but he is from the AEC's," Ben corrected. "As Roger Gladstone told me, Buckeye is Ireland's one and only venture into atomic energy. And while I don't like the man, Ireland's bark is worse than his bite. There have been plenty of times when the Ohio Utility Commission denied him a rate increase, and he hasn't run around murdering them."

Mrs. Westerfeld was wreathed in a smile of satisfaction. "They turned him down last October," she recalled. "Would you believe it, the man wanted a seventy-five per cent fuel adjustment? They gave him twelve and a half, and he stamped out of the hearing threatening to close down his generators."

Val was stirred to philosophy by these reminiscences. "One of the few hassles you're protected from in Congress is setting electricity rates. I don't know how they do it—and get away with their skins whole."

He was joined in a moment of pious gratitude by his fellow legislators. Even Elsie Hollenbach, stout-hearted to a fault, blanched at the thought of perils escaped.

"To the best of my knowledge," Ben said as cautiously as if he were advancing a stupefying conclusion, "nobody has ever been killed because of a rate hearing. Which proves that Ireland doesn't run amuck every time he's thwarted. Because, on the whole, rates are a lot more important to him than one generating station. So we come back to what I was saying. The only suspects to whom these nuclear plants are central are the people at the AEC—and Roger Gladstone. But nobody from the AEC was at the Murren Grange, except for Davis Quentin and he was the victim."

"Just one moment, Ben." Mrs. Hollenbach, having scanned the dessert menu and made her choice, was now at leisure to bear down with her powerful critical faculties. "I grant the general validity of what you say. But when we speak of someone at the AEC killing to protect his future, we are talking, of course, about bribery. That is what he would be trying to hide. And when a federal employee is bribed, a crime has been committed by two people—the taker and the giver. Therefore it is insufficient to say that neither Andrew Heisse nor Jim Vorhees was present in Murren on the night of Inspector Quentin's murder. The same motive could apply to Sheridan Ireland."

Elsie's logic, as usual, was impeccable. Unfortunately, her grasp on reality had momentarily slipped. The hoots of her colleagues recalled her to her senses.

"For God's sake, you know things don't work that way—" Ben began.

"You been sleeping at the switch, Elsie?" rumbled Val Oakes, lofting one disapproving eyebrow.

"Hell, if Heisse took a bribe from Tristate, he'd go to jail, all right. But Ireland would get off with a rap on the knuckles. His company would probably have to fork over a thousand-dollar fine. In fact," Tony nodded his head sagely, "it wouldn't surprise me if they had some experience with paying fines."

Under this combined assault Elsie gave way. Collecting herself she agreed that she had been in error.

Fortified by his triumph Ben expanded the argument. "There's another reason for crossing off bribery as the underlying motive for the killer. What kind of discovery were Quentin and Kennison likely to make? Quentin was an expert on nuclear safety. Kennison was an expert on hydrodynamics. The odds are strong that Quentin would have unearthed a technical flaw rather than financial skullduggery. And again the double murder has its effect. With Kennison dead, those odds became a sure thing. We should have been able to tell right then what happened. Inspector Quentin, on his tour of the Midwest sites, discovered a chronic defect in the Lomax generator. After it had been in operation a while, the coolant system always began to leak. In other words, something was wrong with the design. So he was flying back to Washington to get a stop order issued that would have closed down all the Lomax installations."

Tony Martinelli was always coming up with surprising information. "Might not have finished Lomax," he reflected. "They're a damned big outfit."

"Maybe not. But it sure as hell would have finished Roger Gladstone. Everybody's touchy enough about this area, without hiring a designer who builds in trouble."

Val Oakes, pondering the ruby depths of his glass, had already figured things out for himself. "And then, as was bound to happen, Kennison made the same discovery. So he had to be killed, too."

Lorraine was puzzled and not ashamed to show it. "You make it sound so simple," she said discontentedly, "but that isn't how it looked while it was happening."

"I've stripped away all the underbrush and that's what made it difficult," Ben reassured her promptly. "The Carrs were a godsend to Gladstone. And not only because their PEP rally provided cover for the actual murder in Murren. They kept things hopping afterward with their libel suits and their charges against Tristate. Without them, not half so much attention would have been riveted on Buckeye. And it didn't help to have Heisse and Vorhees hypnotized by their fear of some irregularity within the AEC. Of course, they were already worried because of Nina Yeager's activities. Then Quentin's murder convinced them they were dealing with an inside job."

Elsie Hollenbach remembered that she was a California Republican. "Andy Heisse wouldn't have stayed hypnotized forever."

"Nobody realized that better than Roger Gladstone. When Kennison ordered him to a showdown in Washington, he knew his greatest danger was going to be the parallel between the two victims. So he got busy, diverting attention from the truth."

Tony had spent almost as much time as Ben answering police questions about Humphrey Kennison's death. Consequently, he was well up on its details.

"All those phone calls?" he asked alertly. "They always did sound fishy to me."

"But then almost everything does," Ben grinned. "Yes. Kennison called only Gladstone and the AEC. Then at the last minute he remembered he should warn me against making a fool of myself in public. It was Gladstone who called Ireland's office and Paul Carr's. Without them, it would have looked like a meeting about Lomax Tool. With them, it looked like a meeting about Buckeye Atomic. And as a useful by-product, he got a couple of additional suspects descending on Washington."

"Hmph!" It was a complex, appreciative noise from Val Oakes. "That was clever."

Lorraine did not see it that way. "Was he crazy or something?" she demanded indignantly. "Those reactors are inspected regularly. Was he planning to kill all of Davis Quentin's replacements?"

"All he wanted was a breathing space." Ben sighed as he remembered Gladstone's monotonous reiteration after his arrest. "According to him, he could have corrected the defect in his design. He was going to call it a modification in the Buckeye specs. Then he was going to insist on altering the existing Lomax generators to conform. He thought he could get away with it and not have anyone catch on. In fact, he asked Kennison to let him do it, but without success."

Tony whistled. "You have to hand it to the guy. He bumps off two obstacles, gets the police in an uproar and then sits down calmly to doodle on his blueprints."

"I don't think there was anything calm about him by that time," Ben disagreed. "You see, he knew all the weak points in his position. He was the one who actually left the Murren Grange and got swept back inside, although he never admitted going further than the porch. He was the first person Kennison called to the Washington meeting, and the police knew it. He was telling everybody that Heisse had instigated the Buckeye delay, while Heisse knew that was not so. And, finally, he was the only one who had planned his lack of alibi."

Tony narrowed his eye suspiciously. "None of them had alibis, Ben."

"Agreed. But Ireland could not be sure that George Barry would be late. What if Barry had walked into an empty room at twelve o'clock? And Vorhees couldn't count on Heisse not being available for lunch. For all I know, Heisse couldn't count on Mrs. Heisse not stopping by for something she'd forgotten. But Gladstone had set things up to be alone for two hours. It stood out like a sore thumb. What's more, Gladstone knew it and he didn't like it. He's got the kind of mind that likes to tidy things up. He wanted to fix his reactors without anybody ever knowing something had been wrong. And he wanted to take the teeth out of the police investigation by concentrating all suspicion on another person. That's when he got lucky—he thought!"

Four agile minds had no problem with this.

"Abby Carr!" they chorused.

"Her accusation and Ireland's reception of it," Ben amplified. "Before the smoke cleared, Gladstone was up and about—telling people that Ireland was overreacting. Then, when Ireland objected to the delay in Buckeye, he managed to convince Heisse there was something more sinister than simple egotism in Ireland's rage. In fact, he was so wrapped up in his own schemes he didn't even notice that Sheridan Ireland was solving two murders."

Lorraine Westerfeld could not believe her ears. "Sheridan Ireland!" she gasped. "Are you telling me he figured all this out?"

Ben was almost apologetic. "Well, quite a lot of people have told us that underneath all the bluster he's no fool. Of course, he had the advantage over us of being very aware of where the Lomax reactors were. He'd already figured out that Kennison and Quentin were doing the same sort of thing before they were murdered. Then Heisse let the cat out of the bag and told him that Roger Gladstone was going to the same places. It didn't take more than three drinks for Ireland to see that they all had been tramping around the Lomax generators. After that he had no problem understanding why Gladstone suddenly wanted time to redesign his reactor."

"If he knew all that, why didn't he say so instead of acting like a mental case?" Lorraine cried.

"It's the old business of the boy who cried Wolf! Ireland spends most of his time counterfeiting shock and indignation. When the real thing came along, it rocked him right off his heels. The only thing he could think of doing was rushing over to the Statler to confront Gladstone," Ben theorized.

Val had a simpler explanation. "Nobody ever tells you anything in plain words," he mourned. "You should listen to some of the scientists at our hearings, Lorraine."

"And then . . ." Ben paused and, to forestall the coming explosion, reached over and filled Lorraine's glass. "And then you gave Roger Gladstone the brilliant idea of murdering Sheridan Ireland."

"Me!" The wine she had incautiously sipped sputtered all over her napkin. It was a moment before she emerged from the white linen. "I did not!"

"Oh, yes you did! You marched to the phone and told Gladstone two things. First, you laid it out for him that Ireland had cottoned on to his game. Then, in the same breath, you assured him there was an independent witness willing to swear that Ireland had gone to the Statler to attack him. Gladstone didn't have to be a genius to see how he could close the case for good. All he had to do was stage a fight, wrestle with Ireland for a gun, and shoot him in self-defense."

Lorraine was speechless, her eyes round with horror.

Elsie Hollenbach swung briskly into action. Casting a disciplinary glance at Ben, she began an inquisition. "And is that what happened?"

"Not exactly," Ben admitted. "Gladstone was spoiled. While he'd done a lot of worrying about being caught, in his experience the actual committing of murder was easy. After all, Quentin wasn't expecting violence and Kennison thought he was giving an ex-student a failing mark. Ireland was a different proposition altogether. He went up there thinking of Gladstone as a killer. He says the minute the door closed, Gladstone threw a lamp to the floor and reached for his pocket. Ireland didn't wait to see what would happen. He just hurled himself at Gladstone's throat."

Elsie had turned herself into judge and jury.

"Very well," she said deliberately. "That is Mr. Ireland's story. What does Gladstone say?"

"He says the same thing," Ben reported. "Didn't you know he'd confessed?"

Tony was frankly disappointed. "Hasn't he got any backbone? When the police break in on two guys wrestling on the floor, it's one man's word against the other."

It wasn't often that Ben could correct Tony on details like this. "Not this time. To carry out his plan, Gladstone had to do two things. He had to shoot Ireland at short range and he had to get Ireland's fingerprints on the gun. That's why he was still struggling so desperately, right until Tommy Youngman broke them apart. Gladstone was arrested with the gun that killed Humphrey Kennison in his pocket—and the only fingerprints on it were those of Roger Gladstone!"

Tony threw up his hands disgustedly at this rank amateurism. Lorraine, however, had forgotten her mortification.

"All the papers had Tommy's picture, and did you see James Proctor last night? He mentioned Tommy's name at least three times. Heidi will be so proud."

"I'm glad Tommy has done well," Ben said truthfully, "but he isn't the only one. Sheridan Ireland has come out of this smelling like roses, too."

"You mean that write-up yesterday morning?" Tony scoffed. "All about how he fearlessly confronted a murderer and how he grappled with him and held him until the law showed up?"

"I was thinking of that statement of his today. The one where he says this proves we can't be too careful about the design of our nuclear reactors, and he personally is going to oversee the selection for Buckeye to ensure that Ohio leads the nation in safety."

Lorraine's gurgle of laughter made her the center of all eyes.

"He called me up this morning," she explained. "He was trying to sign me on for his next campaign in Murren."

"And what did you tell him?" Mrs. Hollenbach asked piercingly.

Lorraine was all innocence. "I asked him if he was sure he had the right number. George Barry was the one who took that kind of call."

While Elsie nodded approvingly, Ben asked, "And what will Barry do now that everyone in Murren knows he was being paid off? Leave town?"

"Good heavens, no! He'll just have to live it down." Lorraine struggled to explain. "That may be the real difference between a small town and a city. In a city, if you get caught out, you hightail it. But in Murren, you grin and bear it until people forget."

"You may be right," Ben reflected. "Anyway, that seems to be Nina Yeager's theory. I understand she's leaving for California. Heisse asked for her resignation as soon as he found out what she'd been up to. I don't know why Jim Vorhees is taking her defection as a personal betrayal."

"Ah, these young women!" Val breathed ponderously. "They can cause a lot of ruction in an office."

Lorraine leaned forward confidentially. "Not just in an office," she said with a wealth of meaning.

"Oh?" Val encouraged her.

"About the same time Mr. Heisse found out what was going on, so did Abby Carr. She went back to Newburg without her husband."

Four heads inclined toward her.

"Paul followed on the next plane," Mrs. Westerfeld reported soberly.

"Now there's the best news you've had in a long time, Ben," said Val enthusiastically. "That young man is going to have his hands full without leading ban-the-bomb movements."

"And without running for public office," added Ben, storing up this tidbit for Janet.

Val was automatically preparing to herald the happy event by reaching for the swaddled bottle. "It takes some of these boys a long time to learn that you can't concentrate on politics, until you've established peace on the home front."

Ben was the first to find the toast. "And may they do their learning some place besides Ohio's Fiftieth District!"